Please turn to the back of the book
for a conversation between
Lee Harris and Christine Bennett

I could not exaggerate the shock I experienced at hearing her pronouncement. For a moment it left me short of breath and dizzy. I'm not sure whether there was a fleeting moment in which I thought that what she said might be true or whether I simply felt immediate disgust and anger that anyone would say something so untrue, so impossible to believe, and so impossible to have happened—something that could devastate the life and career of a woman whom I believed to be a paragon of virtue.

"Tina," I said, "I think you should reconsider what you just said. I've known Sister Joseph for most of my life. She is a devout Catholic, a devoted member of the convent, a great leader. She has never had a child."

"Were you there twenty years ago?"

By Lee Harris
Published by Fawcett Books:

THE GOOD FRIDAY MURDER
THE YOM KIPPUR MURDER
THE CHRISTENING DAY MURDER
THE ST. PATRICK'S DAY MURDER
THE CHRISTMAS NIGHT MURDER
THE THANKSGIVING DAY MURDER
THE PASSOVER MURDER
THE VALENTINE'S DAY MURDER
THE NEW YEAR'S EVE MURDER
THE LABOR DAY MURDER
THE FATHER'S DAY MURDER
THE MOTHER'S DAY MURDER

Books published by The Ballantine Publishing Group
are available at quantity discounts on bulk purchases
for premium, educational, fund-raising, and special
sales use. For details, please call 1-800-733-3000.

THE
MOTHER'S
DAY
MURDER

Lee Harris

FAWCETT BOOKS • NEW YORK

Sale of this book without a front cover may be unauthorized. If this book is coverless, it may have been reported to the publisher as "unsold or destroyed" and neither the author nor the publisher may have received payment for it.

A Fawcett Book
Published by The Ballantine Publishing Group
Copyright © 2000 by Lee Harris

All rights reserved under International and Pan-American Copyright Conventions. Published in the United States by The Ballantine Publishing Group, a division of Random House, Inc., New York, and simultaneously in Canada by Random House of Canada Limited, Toronto.

Fawcett is a registered trademark and the Fawcett colophon is a trademark of Random House, Inc.

www.randomhouse.com/BB/

Library of Congress Catalog Card Number: 00-190071

ISBN 0-449-00442-2

Manufactured in the United States of America

First Edition: April 2000

10   9   8   7   6   5   4   3   2

To my daughter, Molly,
who makes being a mother a pleasure
every day of the year

The author wishes to thank Ana M. Soler and James L. V. Wegman for a happy dozen books of help and information, which just get better all the time!

Oh, my son's my son till he gets him a wife,
But my daughter's my daughter all her life.

—Dinah Maria Mulock Craik (1826–1887),
   Young and Old

Prologue

Twenty Years Ago

"I have the papers." The woman named Mrs. Del-Bello was gently rounded and looked starched, although she was not a nurse. "Do you want to read them? I can give you a few minutes."

The other woman seemed unsure. "I suppose I should." She pulled herself up carefully to a sitting position in the hospital bed, wincing slightly, then adjusted the pillow behind her. Sunlight streamed through the single window, exactly hitting the papers on her lap. She looked toward the window, but could see nothing except sky. They were on a high floor, the tallest building in the area. "Just give me a few minutes."

Mrs. DelBello walked quietly out of the room and the woman in the hospital bed pressed the bridge of her glasses closer to her face and read through the document. It was just as it had been explained to her and she had no problems and no complaints. She looked around for a pen but there was none on the table next to her.

A moment later Mrs. DelBello knocked lightly, then opened the door, as though, with experience, she had

1

timed the reading of the document. "Do you have any questions, dear?" she asked.

"I just need a pen."

Mrs. DelBello handed her one from her handbag. "I can witness your signature."

"Thank you."

"Would you like to see her again?"

The woman in the bed swallowed, closed her eyes for a moment, then shook her head. "No, thank you."

"Then I think we've done it."

"The records are sealed, is that right?" She knew the answer but she wanted to hear it one more time. It was the most important question she had asked.

"Sealed forever. None of this will go further than the agency. You can rest assured. And they're a lovely couple. They'll bring her up just the way you would."

"Here's the agreement."

"Thank you. Take it easy, dear. Things will get better."

The woman in the bed nodded and watched Mrs. Del-Bello leave the room for the last time. Then she looked at the window again, at the sky and the brilliant light. It was time to rest, to rest assured.

1

A small crowd had gathered down the block and across the street from my house when I came outside that afternoon with Eddie, my two-and-a-half-year-old. I knew before I got there what it was about, a situation I had shaken my head over more than once during the spring months, wondering at the things that people found to argue over. It would be better not to walk in that direction and get caught in the fracas but Eddie spotted my friend watching from her driveway and said, "Mel. Wanna see Mel," as he took off toward his chief cookie-baker-and-giver and the small angry crowd nearby.

They were actually shouting when we got there.

"Chris, hi," Mel said, scooping up Eddie. "I know what you want."

"A cookie." He said it with the kind of smile Mel found irresistible.

"We'll get you a cookie soon," she said, nuzzling him so that he giggled. "They're going to kill each other over this," she said to me. "Can you believe it's gone this far?"

"Only when I see it."

"Yes, you will," the man at the center of the group was saying in too loud a voice. "And you'll pay for it.

3

You've had ten years to take care of this and you haven't done a damn thing."

"You have no heart," the woman standing nearest him called back. "That's all I can say. You probably drown stray cats, too."

"Enough," Mel said. "Let's go inside and find the cookies and get away from this horror. I hate seeing reasonable people become monsters." She looked around. "Sari? Noah? Come on. We're going in."

The five of us trooped into the house, the children grabbing their cookies and going upstairs, Mel and I hanging around the kitchen until the tea was made and then carrying our snack into the family room.

"Hal talked about moving last night," Mel said after she poured.

"Mel, don't say that. What will I do without you?"

"What will I do? But this is getting crazy. That man has lost his mind and the Greiners won't give an inch. He's probably got the law on his side and I understand his point of view, but it's hard to like him. The Greiners are nice people but they've got to acknowledge they've caused a problem for him. Did you get the flyer in your mailbox?"

"Two flyers. One for and one against. Jack checked with the police, just on a hunch. Do you know Mr. Kovak owns a handgun?"

"What?"

"A pistol. It's all licensed and legal. He doesn't have a permit to carry, just to keep it on the premises."

"That's very scary."

"Lots of people own guns, Mel. It's the world we live in."

"Well, he better not use it over a tree."

It was a tree, in fact, that was the center of the discord on Pine Brook Road, a tree that had turned neighbor against neighbor. However many years ago, a seed from a silver maple had blown from the mother tree and settled on the edge of the Greiners' property, eventually planting itself and becoming a small sapling. I had not lived in Oakwood when that happened, although I had visited my aunt frequently in the house that I inherited from her a few years ago. When the seed rooted, I was a Franciscan nun living upstate in St. Stephen's Convent, not far from the Hudson River. By the time Aunt Meg had died, bequeathing the house to me, and I had been released from my vows and taken up residence on Pine Brook Road, the once tiny and fragile sapling was already a tree. Today, four years later, it was a good-sized tree with pretty, silvery leaves that moved gracefully in the wind and shaded the area beneath, and unfortunately wreaked havoc with Mr. Kovak's driveway only a few feet away from the trunk and just above the most aggressive of the roots.

The upshot of this natural phenomenon was that the Kovaks' driveway, an expensive concrete job, was being raised by the thickening roots. During the winter he had quite a problem getting over the icy hump and he was not happy. His anger had blossomed with the first green leaves of spring. I couldn't blame him. What he wanted from the Greiners was the removal of the tree, the removal of all the roots, and the replacement of the damaged piece of his driveway. The Greiners would have none of it.

"The Greiners could have mowed it down ten years ago when it was a flexible stick with a leaf," I said. "I hate to tell you what Jack mows down by accident."

"He's not the only one." Mel sipped her tea. "You're right. They could have. I'm sure they went to some trouble to preserve it when they saw it. And they should have known it wouldn't stay tiny for long. I mean, if you plant things, you know they're going to grow."

"How did the Kovaks' driveway come to be so close to the property line?" I asked. "The law says you have to leave so many feet between the boundary and whatever you build."

"I heard they got a variance when they built the house because the property was a little smaller than the usual minimum. It just worked out that way and the town gave them the variance because if they didn't, they wouldn't build a house there and the town wouldn't get the taxes and—you see the way they were thinking. The Kovaks have the law on their side."

"But such anger," I said. "Such hostility. Can't the Greiners agree to anything?"

"What's to agree to? If they don't get rid of the tree, the problem will only get worse. Someone even suggested the Kovaks try to move the driveway closer to their house but that's a tremendous expense and who's to say the tree won't send its roots over that way?"

"I hate the way people are taking sides. They need some kind of professional mediator."

"Why don't you volunteer?" Mel gave me a smile. "You got this town out of a hole a couple of years ago."

She was referring to the time when, soon after I had moved in, I was appointed to determine who had murdered a woman in Brooklyn forty years earlier. "I'm not exactly disinterested," I said. "Although to the extent that I can't side with either of them, I guess I am."

"I just hate the bickering," Mel said. "It seems to me,

setting aside which neighbor I like and which one I don't like, that the Greiners should cut the tree down and see if they can negotiate some kind of settlement with the Kovaks. Maybe if they offer to pay half the cost of fixing the driveway, the Kovaks will come around."

It sounded reasonable to me, although I could see that the Kovaks might want full restitution and if they took the case to court, they might get it. "Is there a lawsuit yet?" I asked.

"I don't really know. I'm sure there will be if this isn't settled. If that tree keeps on growing this summer the way it's been growing the last few years, that driveway's going to be a mess when winter comes. I don't know. Mr. Kovak is not a pleasant person but I think he's right in this case."

"I don't know him very well," I said. "What's unpleasant about him?"

"He just seems to be mad at the world. I've said hello to him when I was walking or jogging past the house and he was working outside, and he's practically turned his back on me. Maybe he's had a tough life; I don't know. But it sure looks like this tree is the last straw."

We changed the conversation at that point and when I finally dragged Eddie down from the second floor and went outside, the angry crowd had completely disappeared. I walked the length of the Greiners' property—they were Mel's next-door neighbors—and stood near what appeared to be the property line and looked at the offending tree. It was very pretty, tall and slim, its silvery leaves a pleasure to watch in the breeze. Almost next to it, the driveway had heaved and I could sympathize with anyone who had to drive over it, especially in the winter.

"What're you looking at?" an angry voice asked, and Eddie grabbed my leg and stood close to me.

"The tree and the driveway," I said, trying to exhibit fairness.

"Well, there's nothing to look at. Move on."

I was standing in the street—our block has no sidewalks—and he had no right to ask me to get off town property, but I had no wish to agitate him. "Come on, Eddie," I said, taking his hand. "It's time to go home."

"Is that man mad?" Eddie said.

"I think he's having a bad day, sweetie. He's not mad at us. He's just upset about something."

Eddie dropped my hand and picked up a little stone that lay on the road. He showed it to me with pride and I watched him carefully to make sure it didn't make its way into his mouth. When we got home, he put it down and I got rid of it. Sometimes there are simple solutions to small problems.

Jack, my husband of almost four years, is a cop. When I met him, not long after I left St. Stephen's Convent, he was a detective sergeant with NYPD and he was starting law school. Happily, he not only survived law school—no small feat; he was working full-time and going to school at night—but graduated about a year ago, at which time his career changed dramatically. He left the precinct in Brooklyn where he had worked for several years. For many months after graduating and while studying for the bar, he worked at One Police Plaza, the headquarters building in Manhattan, answering telephone questions from police officers in the field, giving them guidance according to the law when they needed it. Since passing the bar a few months ago, an event that prompted a great celebration in our household, his job has changed yet again. He's still with the Legal Bureau at One PP but now he reads reports concerning unusual police activity called UF 49s, for Uniformed Force, to determine whether the officers involved acted legally. Sometimes these involve shootings or other serious violence, while others are simply police-citizen interactions resulting in complaints of one kind or another.

I am very happy that he is getting this kind of experience. Neither of us knows where he will go from here, whether he will stay with NYPD or go into the practice of law, but everything he learns now will help him make the right decision and make him a better lawyer, wherever he works.

On that day of the tree incident, he was working the ten-to-six shift so I was expecting to eat dinner with him when he got home, probably after Eddie went to bed. I got Eddie's dinner ready and sat with him while he ate. Afterward, I gave him a much needed bath and got him into his pajamas. We were walking back to his bedroom when I heard the doorbell ring.

It was an unusual time for someone to be coming to the door. We don't get many door-to-door salesmen in Oakwood because there are rigorously enforced rules as to who may engage in such selling. And since this was the dinner hour, it would be odd for a neighbor to drop by without telephoning first. I called down the stairs and went down slowly with Eddie.

Before I got to the door, the bell rang again. I pulled the door open and was startled by the person standing in front of me. I had never seen her face before but I recognized what she was wearing. It was the brown habit of a novice at St. Stephen's. The face framed by the veil was young and pale and perhaps just a little frightened.

"Are you Chris?" she asked.

"Yes."

"I'm Tina. I'm a novice at St. Stephen's. I need your help."

There was a frantic edge to her voice that troubled me. "Come in," I said. "This is my son, Eddie. Eddie, this is Tina."

Eddie smiled. Tina looked at him and smiled, too. "He's adorable," she said. "Hi, Eddie."

"Hi."

"Eddie's getting ready for bed now," I said. "Could you give us about ten minutes?"

"Yes."

"You can sit in the family room." She dropped a stuffed duffel bag on the floor near the door and I led her there, walking through the kitchen to the back of the house. "You can watch TV or read. There are magazines and newspapers."

"Thank you." She sat at one end of the sofa, her spine very straight, and closed her eyes.

"I'll be down soon." I picked up Eddie and took him upstairs, wondering what on earth this was all about. There had been no car parked in front of my house and where we live, if you don't come by car, you just don't get here. I could not believe that this girl had walked from a bus or train station.

I read Eddie a story and put him in his crib. He was starting to get big for the crib but he still fit and I was happy to leave things as they were for a little while longer. He turned over and I covered him with a light blanket. "Good night, sweetie pie," I said.

He mumbled something that was probably good night and I left the room.

My guest was sitting on the sofa, staring straight ahead as though I had left her ten seconds ago instead of ten minutes. When I sat opposite her, she seemed to come to life.

"Can I get you anything?" I asked, trying to be a good hostess and putting off my questions.

"No, thank you. I have a problem and I don't know who to turn to. I need your help."

"I'll do what I can. What's the problem?"

She took a deep breath and her whole body quivered. "It's Sister Joseph," she said, speaking the name of the Superior at St. Stephen's and my dearest friend. "I don't know how to tell you this so I'll just say it and you'll see what the problem is. Sister Joseph is my mother."

2

I could not exaggerate the shock I experienced at
hearing her pronouncement. For a moment it left me
short of breath and dizzy. I'm not sure whether there
was a fleeting moment in which I thought that what
she said might be true or whether I simply felt immediate
disgust and anger that anyone would say something so
untrue, so impossible to believe and so impossible to
have happened—something that could devastate the life
and career of a woman whom I believed to be a paragon
of virtue.

"Tina," I said, "I think you should reconsider what
you just said. I've known Sister Joseph for most of my
life. She is a devout Catholic, a devoted member of the
convent, a great leader. She has never had a child."

"Were you there twenty years ago?"

I did some simple subtraction. "No, I wasn't. I came
there a little after that." I had been fifteen, orphaned,
unable to remain with my aunt and uncle. Joseph had
been my friend and my adviser, almost an older sister. I
had survived those first terrible months because she had
dedicated herself to my survival and to my happiness.

"I'm twenty," the girl sitting on my sofa said. "I can
tell you where I was born. I can tell you who adopted

me. You can talk to them. They'll confirm that they're my adoptive parents."

"But you can't show me any records with Sister Joseph's name on them."

"Not right now. But they exist. She gave birth to me twenty years ago and if you give me some time, I can prove it to you."

"How did you get here, Tina?"

"I took the train and then got a taxi."

I was starting to feel very uncomfortable. I knew she was going to ask me if she could stay overnight. Since the birth of my son two and a half years ago, I have become very careful and cautious. If this young woman was paranoid I didn't want her staying in the same house as my child. But how could I throw her out on the street? "Where did you get the money for the train and the taxi?" I asked. I know how little money nuns and novices have access to. When I made my monthly trips to Oakwood, I needed special permission and money was taken out of my dowry to pay the expenses.

"My parents send me money. It's mine. I didn't steal it." She had a pouty look as she spoke and there was defiance in her voice.

"Does Sister Joseph know you're here?"

"No. *No!* Please don't tell her." She looked as if she might cry.

"I'm not telling her anything. But I think you have a lot of explaining to do. I need to know why you're here, whether you got permission to leave St. Stephen's, who you are, what the problem is, and what you expect from me." I looked at my watch. "But there isn't time now. My husband is coming home soon and I've got to get dinner ready. Will you join us?" I tried to sound pleasant and inviting, neither of which I felt.

"Thank you, I'd like that. And I can help with dinner."

"That's all right. There isn't much to do." I felt myself somewhat disarmed by her offer. I told her she could stay where she was or use the bathroom. As soon as my husband arrived, we would eat.

"Thank you," she said. "I need your help, Chris. I really do."

Jack came home a little while later and I went outside to greet him and tell him about our visitor.

"I don't like this," he said. "You should call Sister Joseph and find out what's going on."

"I can't do that yet. I've promised her I'll listen to her story. As crazy as it may be."

"That's your call. She staying the night?"

"We haven't discussed it but I don't see I have much of a choice."

"You always have a choice. If push comes to shove, you can call Father Hanrahan and ask if she can stay at the rectory."

"I hadn't thought of that. Let's have dinner and let me listen to whatever she wants to tell me. Then I'll decide."

He put his arm around me and we walked inside. Tina was sitting where I had left her but she jumped to her feet to say hello to Jack. He responded somewhat curtly and went upstairs to change. By the time he came down, I had the table set for three and the thermometer in my roast beef was within the acceptable range.

"Thank you both very much," Tina said, sitting down at the table. "I haven't eaten since breakfast."

"That must be over twelve hours ago," I said.

"It was."

"Well, there's plenty of meat so don't be shy."

We kept the conversation away from Tina, Jack talking about a new case he was reviewing, one that looked iffy for the police officers on the scene. He was afraid they hadn't given the proper warnings and that they might not have used their weapons justifiably. As always, I could see how he was torn between what he knew to be legally correct and wanting to defend the officers, who had been in a very dangerous situation.

As he knew from personal experience, police officers are often required to make instant decisions involving the use of their weapons, which after review in a calmer, less dangerous setting appear to be overreaction or unnecessary, and sometimes can cross the line into actual criminal activity.

Tina contributed little to the conversation. If anything, she seemed confused. She ate heartily and helped me clear the table when we were finished.

After the dishes were done, I suggested she and I sit in the living room, a room we hardly use since adding a huge family room to the back of the house before Eddie was born. Jack retired there with a whispered "Don't make any promises," and Tina and I went to the front of the house and got comfortable.

I didn't say anything, but I recalled a visit to St. Stephen's about a year ago when I had had a long talk with Sister Joseph. At that time she told me how few novices had entered the convent and that she had her doubts about one of them. No names had been mentioned but I wondered whether this was the one she had referred to.

I was troubled and starting to regret allowing myself

to get into a situation where I was about to hear things I did not want to hear from a person whose credibility was shaky at best. Finally I looked up and saw Tina sitting like a statue on the sofa, as though waiting for permission to speak.

"Why are you here, Tina?" I asked, just to get her going.

"I need your help and I'm afraid."

"Afraid of what?"

"I'm afraid of her."

"Tina, you are speaking of someone I have known, loved, and trusted for more than half my life. I can imagine fearing her anger if I had done something reprehensible, but otherwise, she is not a person who inspires fear. You'll have to explain yourself or I will ask you to leave." I tried to sound stern, as though I were talking to one of my students who had not delivered a paper, although something about Tina touched me.

"I'm afraid of her because I think she's guessed who I am and she doesn't want the truth to come out. She gave birth to me twenty years ago when she was in her twenties. She was living and working in Ohio at that time, and after I was born she went back to St. Stephen's. She gave me up for adoption when I was just a few days old."

"I would think the records would have been sealed," I said.

"They were. But I was able to get a summer job at the hospital. I got into the records."

"What did you find?"

"Sister Joseph's real name and the address she gave when she checked into the hospital. And the name of the agency that gave me to my parents."

I looked at her face, trying to see something of Joseph in it, but I could not. "There's no resemblance between you," I said.

"I have a father, too."

"Do you know him?"

"No. I couldn't find him."

"I take it you haven't spoken to Sister Joseph about this."

"No. I'm very nervous. I want to get to the bottom of this but I need someone to help me."

"Is that the reason you entered St. Stephen's, Tina?"

"I want a religious life. I thought about several convents, but the reason I chose St. Stephen's is probably because of her. I wanted to know her. I wanted to be near her. I wanted to know what kind of person she was."

"And what have you found out?"

"I don't think I want to talk about it."

"Why are you here, Tina?"

"I heard about you. I even saw you once or twice when you came to visit with your little boy. Once I knew your name, it was easy to find your address. It's not hidden; it's in a file. People talked about you, Sister Angela, Sister Dolores in the Villa, some of the others. I knew you had a close relationship with Sister Joseph and that you had left the convent a few years ago. And everyone seemed to like you. I didn't know where to go so I thought I'd come here."

"Why now?" I asked.

"Because—because I think she realized who I am. And there's something about the way she's been acting lately—I know she doesn't want the truth to come out and I started to be afraid."

"What are you afraid of? That she'll ask you to leave St. Stephen's?"

She shook her head. "I'm afraid of much worse. I'm afraid—I can't say it."

"Tina, what you're telling me is very improbable. Sister Joseph has been at St. Stephen's more than twenty years."

"She left for a year. I think she took a secular job. I don't know if that's where her family lived, but she went out to Ohio and stayed there for about a year. I don't know whether she was pregnant when she went or whether she got pregnant while she was there. I just know she had a baby and it was me."

I found the conversation so unsettling that I wanted to call it quits and ask her to stop talking. More than that, I wanted her to leave my house and never return and to take with her all the things she had told me so that I would never have to think about them. But I knew none of this was possible. I assumed this girl was unbalanced in some way but I had to press on, to prove to her and to myself that what she was saying was totally without truth.

"Tina, I have known Sister Joseph much longer than I know you. I love her as a friend, I admire her as a human being and as a nun. It seems to me that the only way this can be resolved is for me—or us—to talk to her about your allegations."

"If you could help me—that would really be great. But I need a little time. I've done some stupid things."

"How would you like me to help you?"

"Please don't talk to her until I say it's OK," she pleaded.

"That's fine."

"Maybe we could—we could go together."

I hated the idea of being part of something that I knew was wrong and false, but at the same time, I wanted to put this story of hers to rest. Before she talked to anyone else, I wanted Joseph to have the chance to have her say. "I can do that," I said.

"Just not right now. I'm really a wreck about this. I need some time to think and decide what to do. I feel safe here. If I could stay a day or two, maybe I could decide what to do next."

"You can stay," I said, knowing Jack would not be happy about this, "but if you can't come to a decision, we'll have to get counseling for you."

"Thank you, Chris."

"Would you like to call your parents?"

"No. I don't need to."

"Won't they be worried if someone from St. Stephen's calls and says you've left?"

"No. I've taken care of that."

I couldn't imagine how she could have "taken care of" telling her parents unless she lied to them, but I didn't want to press her, partly because I didn't want her to multiply the lies. "We have a guest room upstairs you can stay in. I suggest you continue your morning and evening prayers. And I think you should spend as much time as possible trying to resolve your problems. I'm here if you want to talk to me."

"Thank you. You're very kind."

"Do you want to return to St. Stephen's as a novice?" I asked. It would be a difficult situation at best, but I wondered if she had thought about it.

"I'm not sure. What are you going to do?"

I wasn't quite sure what her question meant but it put me on the spot. "I'm going to try to find out the truth."

"But you won't talk to Sister Joseph till I'm ready."

"I promise."

"I'd like to go to my room now." She got up and went to the front door where she had left her duffle bag, which was so stuffed that the seams were stretched. She picked it up and followed me up the stairs to the room I had used when I visited Aunt Meg for so many years and which Jack and I now used as a study. But Jack's bar exams were behind him and I wasn't doing any work at the moment for my friend Arnold Gold, the attorney, so Tina could have her privacy.

"This is very nice," she said politely. "Is it all right with you if I just go to bed now? I've been up since five and I'm very tired."

Five was the hour the nuns at St. Stephen's normally awoke. "Whatever you'd like. There's an alarm clock next to the lamp. You're welcome to get up whenever you want."

"Thank you."

"Good night, Tina."

"Good night. Thank you for letting me stay."

3

I stopped in to look at Eddie, who was sleeping peacefully. Then I went downstairs to where Jack was sitting in the family room surrounded by newspapers, a magazine, and some papers that looked like they came from work. He looked up and came as close as I had ever seen him to scowling.

"There's something in her eyes, Chris. This gal's not all there."

"I told her she could stay a couple of days. She's gone to bed. I feel more upset than I've felt in years."

"I'm not surprised. You want to talk about it?"

"I have to. My head is going around in circles."

He pushed the papers off to the side. "How 'bout we have some coffee and put our heads together?"

I agreed. I went to the kitchen and started making the coffee. I didn't want to believe Tina's fantastic story but it nagged at me. I had known Sister Joseph since long before she became the Superior of St. Stephen's. She had been my spiritual director when I came to the convent at the age of fifteen and with time she had become my best friend. She never spoke much about her past or about her family and I had never asked. What business was it of mine where she came from or who her parents were? I knew all that was necessary and relevant and I had learned it by knowing her. It was possible she had come from Ohio and it was equally possible that she came from Missouri. It was possible her parents were living, but I thought it likely that they had died when I was young and new at the convent and the nuns protected me from unpleasant news. The truth is, I remembered no time that Joseph had left for any kind of family matter. Nor did I recall that she was ever mysteriously gone for any length of time.

"Smells good," Jack called from the family room and I came back from my thoughts to the kitchen I was standing in.

I took out the cups and saucers and found some cookies I had tucked away for him and put them on a plate. He came in and filled the cups and carried them back to the family room.

"You didn't tell me much before," he said when we were sitting. "But I can tell you this little gal is not your normal teenager. She's a nervous wreck. What did she tell you?"

I went over it quickly. There wasn't much, as I thought about it, no proof for her accusation, just the promise that she had such proof, just enough to upset me.

"Chris, honey, I can see what this has done to you. You're too sensible to listen to this girl and take anything she says seriously. I don't know if she's out to hurt you or to hurt Sister Joseph, but she's not credible. Believe me. I've heard them all."

Which was true. Until he had graduated from law school last year, he had worked most of his career in a precinct, handling crimes that included homicides. I couldn't guess how many hours of his life had been spent interviewing suspects and witnesses, but the number would be huge. Also, he had met Sister Joseph and, like me, he found her to be an admirable human being.

"What do you think I should do?" I asked, a question I didn't ask very often.

"You want the truth? I think you should just forget everything this kid has told you, point her in the direction of the convent, and wash your hands of this. Chris, you know Sister Joseph. What this girl says happened didn't happen."

I knew he was right and I felt better hearing him say it out loud. "Why would she make up a story like this?"

"Because of her own troubles. She needs something, she wants something. She thinks she can get it by spreading this garbage."

"I told her she should get counseling," I said.

"You're right. But she can't get it here. She has to go back to St. Stephen's or back to wherever her home is and work out what's bothering her. And you're not the one who can help her."

He was giving me good advice, advice that I had asked him for. It remained to be seen whether I would take it, but for the moment I felt better. He went back to the kitchen and got the rest of the coffee.

"You still thinking about it?" he said as he poured.

"I'll be thinking about it for a long time. Even if nothing Tina says is true, it bothers me that she thinks it's true and that she can tell this terrible story to anyone at any time."

"I see what you mean."

"I want to put it to rest. I want to stop her. I don't want these lies to go any further."

"I don't see how you can stop her. You can't lock her

up. Even if she goes back to wherever she came from, she can still talk."

"I know."

"Sleep on it, Chris. There's a great old movie on TV tonight. I haven't seen it in years. You up for it?"

"As long as it's diverting."

"Then let's watch."

I have no idea what the name of the movie was or who was in it. I sat with my eyes turned toward the screen but I probably didn't see any part of it. I kept thrashing Tina's insinuations over in my mind, trying to think of a way that I could prove her wrong without talking to Joseph and embarrassing them both. The problem was, the only people I knew who knew Joseph were nuns at the convent, and I couldn't ask any of them.

I literally went through every nun in my head while I sat there, considering whether I could pose an indiscreet question, or at least a question about an indiscreet happening. I knew I couldn't ask Angela, one of the nuns I was friendliest with and who runs the switchboard, knows where everyone is, how to reach nuns who are away, and whom to inform if some disaster occurs. Angela is younger than I by several years so there was no chance she would have any firsthand knowledge of something that might have happened twenty years ago. I made a short list of nuns I might ask but I wasn't sure how I would handle it.

There had to be some family name in the file for Joseph, but there was no way I was going up to the convent to slink around and peer into documents that were none of my business. If I were investigating someone else, if the source of the information was a secular company, I might do something like that. In fact, I've probably done it already. But this was different. This was St. Stephen's. This was Joseph, General Superior of the convent.

"Still does it to me," Jack said, and I jumped. On the screen in black and white, names were rolling by. Two hours had somehow elapsed since I promised to watch the movie.

"Does what?" I asked, giving him a squeeze.

"Tugs at the old heartstrings."

I rubbed my cheek against his, feeling the stubble at the end of a long day. "Come on up and I'll tug at them."

"No news?"

"I don't care about the news. I want you."

"That's an invitation I can't turn down."

We went upstairs, both of us looking in on Eddie who was sound asleep. Then I quietly turned the knob of the door to the room where Tina was staying. It was very dark inside but she was in bed, her head turned away from me. I listened to her breathing for a moment, then backed out.

I had better things to do.

I had a rocky night. I kept waking up and thinking of how I was going to prove Tina wrong, trying to think of whom I could ask, knowing there wasn't anyone at the convent I could approach. Each time I awoke, I listened for sounds, for someone walking around, but it was very quiet. Suddenly, something came to me in a dream. I almost spoke out loud, I was so happy to have thought of it.

I had gone to live at St. Stephen's when I was fifteen, becoming a novice a few years later when I was old enough. At that time there was a nun there named Sister Jane Anthony, a woman at least ten years older than I and very worldly from my point of view. She had a good secular education, she had friends around the country who used to call her in the evening. I remember thinking that I had almost no one who called me except Aunt Meg and I admitted to being somewhat envious of Sister Jane Anthony. She smoked, too, usually out of doors while sitting in an ungainly position at the foot of a tree or on a rock when the weather was warm or while walking one of the many beautiful paths through the winter snow. If you walked behind her, you might see little holes in the snow where her ashes had dropped.

Her departure from St. Stephen's was so abrupt that it took me a couple of days to realize she was gone. No one said anything, at least not to me, which made me think there was something mysterious and perhaps not completely acceptable about her leaving. I asked one or two of the nuns and got comments that led me to believe we were all better off with Sister Jane Anthony gone.

I knew her last name because she had once told me. It was Cirillo and she had the coloring to go with an Italian name—dark eyes and a wisp of dark hair that sometimes showed outside her veil. I knew, too, that she had gone to New York, because mail that arrived for her had to be readdressed and that was one of my daily charges, along with distributing mail to the nuns' cubbies, for a period of time after she left. Tomorrow morning I would look her up in the directories Jack kept on hand.

My mornings are usually quite busy. I have a toddler to take care of and a husband to feed. I didn't think about Tina till Jack had left and Eddie had eaten his ce-

real, drunk his juice and milk, and clamored to get out
of his feeding table. Then I looked at my watch, decided
it was time for everyone else in the household to get up,
and went upstairs. I knocked on Tina's door and didn't
get a response. I called, "Tina? Are you up yet?" and
knocked again.

A muffled response came from inside.

"Time to get up," I said.

"Oh. Sorry. I guess I overslept. I'll be down in a few
minutes. Is your husband still here?"

"He's gone."

"Good."

I knew what she meant. If only I were home, she could
come down in her robe or nightgown. If Jack was still
here, she would have to dress. I had fixed up the bathroom for her, covering the mirror as my aunt had covered it for me all the years that I visited here. I had set out
towels and a wash cloth and made sure the sink and
bathtub were good and clean. Eddie uses that bathroom
and his etiquette still leaves something to be desired.

I went downstairs and set a place for her. A few minutes later, she came down and sat at the kitchen table.

"Thank you. This looks very nice."

"Anything special you'd like? Eggs? An English
muffin?"

"An English muffin sounds wonderful." She sounded
very enthusiastic, as though it were a special treat.

I had made extra coffee and when the muffin was
ready, I poured for both of us. I enjoy a last cup of coffee
after the morning whirlwind is over and I decided to
take it with Tina.

Since she had overslept, I knew she had not said her
morning prayers, but it wasn't up to me to keep her in

line. Having left St. Stephen's, she might well never go back. It was surely one of the things she was going to think about.

"I have plans for today, Tina," I told her as she buttered her muffin.

"Sure."

"Eddie and I will be gone for several hours. Can you stay alone or is there something you'd like to do?"

"I think I'd like to be alone. Is that all right with you?"

"It's fine. I'll be leaving within the hour. I can leave you a can of tuna for your lunch. There's celery and mayonnaise in the refrigerator, milk, juice, coffee—whatever you'd like. Do you think you'll be going out?"

"What do you mean? Like for a walk?"

"Yes."

"I don't know. Do I need a key?"

"Not if you stay close to home." Actually, we lived in a pretty safe area but I'm married to a policeman and he has great concerns about security, especially where his family is involved.

"I might go out back, if that's all right with you. I just want to think in quiet."

"Out back is fine. There are chairs to sit on and no one will see you."

"Good. I'll do that."

My plans for the day were to drop off Eddie at my babysitter, Elsie Rivers, who is a kind of surrogate grandmother for Eddie, having been my mother's dearest friend when I was a child. I was then going into New York to see if I could talk to Sister Jane Anthony. Before I woke Tina, I had found a J. A. Cirillo in the phone book for Manhattan. The address was in the West Village. I had called the number and a woman had answered on the second ring. I made up my mind, not with the most complete information, that she probably didn't go off to work or she would have left by the time of my call. I might well be wrong but if she wasn't there, I had time to kill and I could talk to the superintendent of her building or the doorman, as the case might be.

"Chris?"

I was slightly startled from my thinking. "Can I get you something?"

"Are you going to see Sister Joseph today?"

"No, I'm not. I told you I wouldn't till you decided what you want to do."

"Thank you." She smiled a quick smile. "I guess you have other things in your life besides my problems."

I smiled back without answering. She was right; I did. But not today, and I didn't want to tell her that.

4

When I left the house, Tina was dressed, her bed was made, and the sun was shining. On the way to the car, I showed her where the outdoor chairs were and helped her set one up on the grass. She assured me she would be fine and I had the feeling she was relieved that I wasn't going to be around. I got Eddie into his carseat, and we took off.

It was after eleven when I got to the address for J. A. Cirillo. The building was old and large. I rang her bell but there was no answer. A man came out of the lobby as I stood outside waiting and he held the door for me, but I refused to go in. If she wasn't home, I would ring the super's bell and see what I could find out from him. I pressed her bell once more and started looking for the super's bell when the buzzer sounded. I dashed over, pushed the door open, and went inside.

Like many old buildings, it was dark inside. I found the elevator and took it upstairs. In contrast to the rest of the building, it was new and practically sailed up the shaft. I got off on five and found her apartment. She hadn't asked who was ringing when I was downstairs so I didn't know what to expect. A moment later she opened the door and I knew I had found the right person.

She frowned. "Who are you? I was expecting someone else."

"I was Sister Edward Frances at St. Stephen's. I'd like to talk to you."

She nodded slowly. "That's weird. Yes, I remember you, the little girl who came in from the cold. Come in. I don't know how long I can talk to you. Who gave you my address?"

"I found it in the phone book." I walked into her living room, which looked as though my son had used it and forgotten to put away his toys. But there was a chair to sit on and Jane Anthony sat on the sofa and lit a cigarette.

"I gather you're not at St. Stephen's anymore either."

"I left a few years ago."

"I remember you very well. You came to us on a dark and stormy night."

I smiled. It was an accurate description. "And I stayed for fifteen years."

"Didn't you used to take trips back to your family on a regular basis?"

I was surprised she remembered. "Yes, I did. I have a retarded cousin that I was anxious to keep up with. I see him frequently now. We live in the same town."

"Anyone ever talk about me after I was gone?"

"As a matter of fact, they didn't talk about you at all, at least not to me."

"Well, you were young and delicate. They wanted to keep you pure and unsullied."

"Perhaps."

"Now that we have that out of the way, tell me what you're here for. You didn't come here to chat me up on old times."

"I have a couple of questions to ask you about things

that happened before I got to St. Stephen's. I hope you'll be able to help me."

"Why not? I have a pretty good memory. What's this all about?"

"It's a little complicated," I said, "and I don't want to go into the whole story right now, especially if you're about to have company. I wondered whether you remembered if Sister Joseph left the convent for any period of time."

She got a perplexed look on her face, as though she might not have understood the question. Then she said, "You mean like a few months or so?"

"Yes."

She stared at me as if trying to figure me out. "Strange question," she said. "I'm getting bad vibes. But yes, I think she did. I couldn't tell you the year or how long she went for, but I remember that she took a leave of absence or some such thing."

"Do you know where she went?"

"What's your name now?" she asked. "I don't suppose you're still Edward."

"I'm Chris, Chris Bennett. And I'm married. My married name is Brooks."

"So it was a man." She looked amused.

"It wasn't a man. I met him after I left. I got permission to leave."

"I didn't."

That didn't surprise me. "You just left."

"I just up and walked out." She ground her cigarette into an ashtray loaded with butts. "Never looked back. Never heard from any of them again. Till right now. You're the first."

And obviously I wasn't inquiring about her health. "Are you still Jane?"

"That's what I am, Jane Anthony Cirillo. I never changed. I think I got off on a tangent. What was it you were asking me?"

I glanced at my notes to make sure. "I wanted to know if you remembered where Sister Joseph went when she took time off."

"Where she went, let's see. Somewhere west, I think. I wasn't a personal friend of hers, you know. Why don't you ask her, or aren't you on speaking terms?"

"We are, but I'd like to find out without asking directly."

"That sounds interesting."

"Do you remember if she was visiting family?"

"Family. She was one person up there that didn't talk family. I had sisters and brothers and I talked about them because they were part of my life, but she didn't. She was like—how can I put it?—like she had no one outside the convent."

"But she took vacations," I said. "She went to visit people."

"But she didn't come back with stories."

It was true. You would see Joseph when she returned from a vacation and she always looked happy and well rested, but she never talked about where she had gone and whom she had seen, except for the times that she attended conferences. But that wasn't family.

"You trying to find her family?" Jane asked.

"Not really. I don't even know if she has one. I'm trying to find out where she went when she took that leave, whether she worked for someone, where she lived. I've run into someone who has an interest in knowing that."

"An anonymous someone?" She raised her eyebrows.

"Yes."

"You're really piquing my curiosity. What's Joseph supposed to have done? Screwed up somebody's books?"

"No, nothing like that."

"I'm pretty sure she was gone for more than a few months. She was teaching at the college and they got a replacement for her, so she must have been gone at least a semester."

That made sense. If she had been gone a few weeks or even a month or so, they might have parceled out her teaching among other nuns and not bothered hiring someone new. "I wish I knew where she'd gone," I said. "If you remember, I'd appreciate your calling me. I'll give you my number." I started writing it down.

"Don't expect me to spend much time thinking about this. I was glad to get away from there and it doesn't occupy my thoughts very much. Never did."

"Can you tell me why you left?"

"Why I left is easy. It's why I went there in the first place that I could never figure out. It was an idea that captured my imagination and hung on to me for a long time. I didn't know I'd made a mistake till a long time after. I was sorry about leaving, even if the nuns wouldn't believe it, but I was very relieved to be gone."

"You left so precipitously," I said. "Did something happen to trigger it?"

The doorbell rang at that moment and Jane jumped up and dashed to the kitchen to buzz in her friend. I knew I wouldn't get an answer now, not that she owed me any.

"I guess time's up," she said, coming back to the living room. "I'll be going out now. Any quick questions?"

"I've left my phone number on the coffee table. If you think of where Sister Joseph went, please give me a call. You can call collect, if you like."

She laughed. "If I had to pick a place, I'd say Ohio. How's that?"

"Not bad." I picked up my bag and she opened the door for me. The elevator was just stopping and as I said good-bye, a woman got out. She was about Jane's age, I guessed, quite nice looking, and dressed much more elegantly than Jane, who had been wearing a skirt and blouse with comfortable shoes. This woman was wearing heels with a suit and was carrying what looked to be a fine leather handbag on her shoulder. It was hard to believe they were going to the same place.

"Hi, sweetie," she called as she breezed past me, her perfume wafting through the air. "You're actually ready."

I stepped into the elevator and pushed the L button. The door closed on their conversation and I went down to get my car.

5

It was the Ohio that got me, of course. What were the chances that she would pick the state that Tina had told me Sister Joseph had gone to? Not much better than one in fifty. I now believed that Joseph had taken a leave from St. Stephen's before I arrived there and that she had stayed away for several months. Considering when I had arrived, the leave must have been twenty years ago or more.

It was chilling to think about. I didn't have to believe that what Tina accused Joseph of was true, but I was now convinced that there was some foundation for her story. It was not unusual for nuns to take a leave from a convent. I myself have known several who did it. People are fond of talking about finding themselves. Well, nuns are no different. Nuns have crises of conscience and belief just as the general population does, and one way to come to terms is to change their environment. They may go home and tend a sick parent or sibling, or they may go somewhere to work at a secular job with all that that entails. When the leave is over, many, perhaps most, return to their convent. Some do not.

In my own case, I had a somewhat irregular arrangement that was made to suit my unusual circumstances.

My cousin Gene lived, and still lives, in Greenwillow, a home for retarded adults, and I wanted to make sure our relationship survived. There was no other family member who could care for Gene besides me when my aunt passed on. As it turned out, my leaving St. Stephen's and my aunt's death happened in the same year. Greenwillow is now in Oakwood and I see Gene frequently, much more often than the monthly visits I made when I was a nun.

To my surprise, I had liked Jane Cirillo. Her almost aggressive outgoing personality had daunted me as a young person, but now I found it rather captivating. Above all, she seemed honest. I had not been sure—and still wasn't—about Tina's honesty. But if there were points of agreement in their stories, there was a good chance those were true facts. The question in my mind was where they would lead.

I stopped in a restaurant near the garage where I had left the car and had lunch. As I ate, I thought about my next move. I was troubled that I had seen no taxi or car near the house when Tina arrived and I wanted to check up on that. And I decided, too, to call a friend at St. Stephen's and try to get her to talk about Jane Anthony. I wasn't especially interested in what I would learn about her, but perhaps I could maneuver the conversation to Joseph's leave.

I drove back to Elsie's house to pick up Eddie. I found them cooking in her kitchen, his face nearly coated with chocolate from the nose down. Elsie was enjoying it and Eddie was trying to make his tongue reach out toward his cheeks.

"I can't even kiss you," I said. "You're covered with chocolate."

Eddie giggled. Suddenly he discovered he could touch his face with his hands and lick the chocolate off his fingers.

"What a mess," I said.

"He deserves something sweet," Elsie said. "He's been very good."

I've never heard Elsie say anything else, but I appreciate her kindness. I asked her if I could use her phone while she got Eddie cleaned up and I went to her sun room and called the taxi company at the station.

"One of your taxis brought a friend to my house yesterday and she thinks she forgot to give him a tip," I said. "I wonder if you could find the driver for me."

"What's your address, miss?" the gruff-voiced man at the other end asked. "I'll check the trip sheets."

I gave him my address, told him she might have gotten off a block away, gave him the time she arrived, and said, "She's a young nun. You may have seen her."

"A nun? Here in the station? Haven't seen a nun here for months. Maybe years. But I'll check."

I waited, hearing paper rustle, listening in on an incoming call for a taxi, and then I was put on hold.

Finally he came back to me. "There's nothing here for any address anywheres near where you live. I just asked the drivers in the station and no one saw a nun or took a nun. Sorry I couldn't help you."

Funny, I thought. She sure didn't walk from St. Stephen's and it's hard to believe she hitchhiked.

*　*　*

Tina was sitting out back when I pulled up the driveway. "There's Tina," I said. We got out and she came to greet us.

"It's been a lovely day," she said. "Your phone rang a few times but I decided to let the machine answer."

"Good. I'll check my messages. Are you hungry?"

"Oh no. I had a good lunch. I used some of the tuna and made a salad. It's very comfortable here, Chris, very restful."

It wasn't restful for me but I had a two-and-a-half-year-old, a substantial difference in our lives. I took Eddie inside and I listened to my messages. Nothing was very important, so I got Eddie happy with some toys and I called St. Stephen's.

Angela usually answers the phone but this time, Sister Grace was on bells. Grace is a talented embroiderer and has made some of the most beautiful altar cloths I have ever seen. She is also older than both Angela and I and I knew she had been at St. Stephen's more than twenty years.

"I ran into someone you may remember," I said, after we had done with our preliminaries. "Sister Jane Anthony?"

"Oh my. That's a name out of the past. You saw her?"

"Yes. We didn't talk long. I remember when she left but I never knew why. All she said was that the question was why she entered St. Stephen's, not why she left."

"That sounds about right. She didn't really fit in, Kix." Grace is one of the people who occasionally still call me by my old nickname. "I used to wonder why she chose a religious life, although she did her part when she was here."

"She's just the same," I said. "Very direct."

"You might say tactless."

"No, just very honest. She didn't say anything nasty about anyone, I promise you."

"Not that it would matter. What's she doing now?"

"She never said. We talked mostly about the old days, even about things that happened before I got there and when I was too young to know what was going on. Did she ever teach in the college?"

"I think she did. Math. She was good at that."

"She seems to have a quick mind," I said. "She remembered several nuns and she asked about Joseph. She was talking about when Joseph took a leave of absence, I guess before I got to St. Stephen's."

"Yes, that was a long time ago. She went to Ohio to take care of a sick friend or relative, I think. I bet that's twenty years ago," Grace said. "It feels like yesterday."

"Well, I never knew about it. She was at St. Stephen's when I got there."

"She came back when the crisis was over. I remember that. She seemed sad when she came back. And she never talked about it. I think she really began to get back to herself when you got here. That's almost twenty years now, isn't it?"

"Almost."

"And a lot has changed. When are you coming to visit your old friends, Mrs. B?"

"Maybe soon," I said. "The spring semester is almost over. I have to write a final for my students. When that's out of the way, I'll give you a call."

"We miss you. And your little sweetheart."

"My little sweetheart is sticky from chocolate."

Grace laughed. "Well, that's just the way a little boy should be. Give him my share, too."

I got off the phone a few minutes later, having sent regards to several of the nuns. I was sitting at the kitchen table, more or less alone. Eddie was on the floor in the family room and I could see him by cocking my head. Tina, I assumed, was outside. That gave me a rare moment to collect my thoughts. Ohio, on leave from St. Stephen's, caring for a sick friend. Had Tina perhaps invaded the convent's files and dug out this information? Had she then concocted the terrible tale she had told me? And if so, why?

I admit I was shaken by the confirmation of Tina's information, but I did not believe that Joseph had had sex or given birth while she was a nun. She and I had never discussed the physical feelings that women, including women in convents, experienced, and I had no intention of starting now. But I knew her. I might not know her family or her secular friends, but I knew this woman and I would vouch for her veracity and her chastity. I had to find out who Tina was and who her natural mother was, or Tina and her stories could prove dangerous.

6

I said nothing to Tina about her problems. She came inside while I was giving Eddie his dinner and she watched as he ate, fascinated with his behavior. It was as though she had never seen a small child up close. Actually, I hadn't seen much of babies and small children when I gave birth, having entered St. Stephen's at the age of fifteen with a minimum of baby-sitting experience.

"Will your husband be home for dinner?" she asked.

"Dinner will be whenever he gets here. With the job he's doing now, he usually arrives between seven and seven-thirty. Eddie can't wait that long for dinner so he gets fed first. I'm going to make my stir-fry tonight. It doesn't take long to cook so I can start it when I hear Jack coming up the drive."

"That sounds good. Uh, I said my evening prayers while I was outside."

I had the feeling she was apologizing for missing her morning prayers by oversleeping. "I always enjoyed evening prayers," I said noncommittally.

"And I think I've decided something." She stopped and watched Eddie for a moment. "I think I'll be leaving here on Sunday."

"OK." I didn't want to ask her destination. "Will you need a ride somewhere?"

"The train. I'm going back to St. Stephen's. I'll call them tomorrow and let them know."

"Would you like me to drive you up there? The train is long and complicated."

"I know. But Sunday is Mother's Day, isn't it? You'll probably want to be with your family."

As it happened, my in-laws were taking a vacation or we would surely have arranged to visit them. "We could go to early mass and I could drive you up and be back home in the afternoon. Jack is either cooking or taking me out to dinner. He won't say. Either way, I can be back in time."

"He's very nice, your husband."

"Thank you. I think so, too."

"If you really think you could, I'd appreciate it."

"Tina, if you want me to go with you to Sister Joseph, I will."

She pressed her lips together and her eyes filled. "Maybe we'll do that," she said. "If I get up my courage by Sunday. If not, I'm going to talk to Father Kramer. I think that may be the place to start."

Father Kramer was the priest who celebrated mass and heard confessions for the convent. I had known him for years and liked him. Although I wasn't happy at the thought of Tina telling him her story—I didn't want anyone to hear the story—I was sure he would keep her confidence. "I think that's a good idea," I said. "It sounds as though you've really been doing some productive thinking."

"I have. Your backyard really helped."

I was glad to hear it. When I took Eddie upstairs for his bath and story, I left Tina to slice up the vegetables.

Eddie fell asleep while I was reading to him so I tucked him in and went downstairs. The vegetables lay on a sheet of wax paper, organized in groups and looking colorful, the peppers red, the snow peas bright green, the mushrooms their usual drab brown-gray. Tina had done a careful, thorough job.

I told her so, then put up the rice. She set the table for me, then sat in the family room, doing nothing. Jack came home a little while later and we all ate, talking about other things. When we finished, Tina helped with the dishes, then excused herself and went upstairs.

"She seems in a better mood," Jack said.

"She's decided to go back to St. Stephen's on Sunday and I'm going to drive her. I'll go to early mass and be back in the afternoon, if that's OK with you."

"Fine. Give me a little time to hone my culinary skills."

"She's going to talk to Father Kramer," I said. "I don't like the idea of his hearing her story, but at least he'll keep it to himself."

"I think that's a very good idea. And he's a good person for her to talk to. Tell me what happened in New York."

I did, and it didn't take long because my visit with Jane Anthony was fairly short.

"She sounds like something else."

"She is. But what seems clear is that Joseph did take a leave and did go to Ohio. I talked to Sister Grace afterward and she confirmed it. She didn't like Jane Anthony much and she didn't do much to hide her feelings."

"Will you talk to Sister Joseph?"

"I don't know. I think I'd like to do some digging on my own first."

"Where are you going to start?"

I looked at my watch. "Tina should still be up. I'm going to ask her for some details that I can try to check. If they don't check out, there's nothing to her story. If they do, I'll decide where to take it."

"Sounds good. I'll put the coffee on and you can go upstairs and do your sleuthing."

I took my notebook and pen and went upstairs. From outside her room, I could hear Tina humming. I knocked and she opened the door.

"May I come in for a minute?"

"Sure. I was just looking for a book on your shelf to read." She was already in her nightgown, a demure one with sleeves and buttons down the front.

I sat on the desk chair. "I'd like you to give me some information, more detailed information than you've given me so far."

"OK."

"The name of the hospital where you were born."

"Good Samaritan."

"The date of your birth."

"May twenty-second."

"The names of your parents."

She paused for a moment. "Anne and Herbert Richmond."

"Their address."

She gave it to me, complete with the zip code. "Are you going to call them?" She looked worried.

"Not without your permission."

"I'd rather they not be involved until I've settled this."

"I respect that. You seem to be afraid that Sister Joseph will take action against you because of what you claim. I'd like to give you my assurance that she would never do that."

"Just please don't say anything to her before I'm ready."

"I promise. The name of the adoption agency."

"God's Love Adoptions. I don't have their address but they're in Cincinnati. They're in the phone book."

"Anything else, Tina? Any name, any date, any fact you can think of that would help me?"

She gave me the date she was adopted, five days after her birth. She didn't recall where her parents were living at that time, but she was sure it was in the file at God's Love.

"Have you seen the file?" I asked.

"I was given information from it. I may have seen a page."

"Who gave you this information?"

"It was the woman who handled the adoption. She was with my birth mother when she signed the papers."

"What's her name?"

"Mrs. DelBello. I don't know her first name. She may have retired by now, but I'm sure she's still around."

7

Jack agreed that the names and dates could prove to be a lot of help. Since tomorrow was Saturday, I wouldn't get to any inquiries for a few days and I didn't want to talk to Joseph until I knew more, or at least until more that Tina had told me had been confirmed, which might never happen.

The question of Tina's taxi ride to our house from the station evoked a raised eyebrow. Although there were reasonable explanations for the ride not appearing on a trip sheet—the driver might have decided to do it off the books—it was troubling to both Jack and me. If Tina had arrived by train, how had she gotten to our house? The duffle bag she carried with her was heavy and the distance was fairly great. It was one of the open questions I would keep thinking about.

On Saturday I visited my cousin Gene at Greenwillow, taking Eddie with me. I often take Gene to mass on Sunday but tomorrow would be hectic and I didn't want to rush him or make him feel he wasn't included in the day's events.

In the afternoon, I ran into my friend, Melanie Gross, as Tina, Eddie, and I were walking down Pine Brook Road. She invited us in and Tina went, although she was

47

hesitant and uncomfortable. I wasn't sure why, but then, Tina was largely a mystery to me.

"I think they may be hiring a professional mediator to decide what should be done about the tree and the fallout from the tree," Mel said. She turned to Tina and gave a quick wrap-up of the problem.

"That sounds like real progress," I said. "Will both families abide by the decision?"

"I don't know. I just heard about it this morning from someone down the street."

"I can't believe this is such a problem," Tina said, clearly surprised.

"We can't either," Mel said. "But it is. Two families that live next door to each other are on the warpath over it, and if they don't come to terms, no one is sure where it's going to end."

"This seems like such a trivial matter. Don't these families know there are hungry children and homeless people within a few miles of here?"

"I'm sure they do," Mel said. "And I'm sure they're concerned. But what's close to people is what gets them riled up. You should see how angry parents can become when their children fail a test or write an essay that's hardly distinguishable as English. They're afraid their little darling won't get into Harvard."

We talked about that for a while and then the three of us started down the block.

"Chris, you have to do something about this," Tina said as we walked.

"About what?"

"This tree problem. I love trees, but I don't see how people can become so enraged about a little tree, even if it's done some damage."

"There isn't much I could do," I said. "I'm not a close friend of either of the families and if a mediator can't get them together, I don't think I'd be able to."

"There has to be something." She patted Eddie's head and he looked up at her and smiled. "We should think about it really hard."

"Do you have any ideas?" I asked.

"No. But it's crazy for people to act like enemies when they're neighbors. And everyone seems to accept it."

Although she was probably including me in her "everyone," I didn't respond because I didn't want to get into a discussion without end again. We all ate together and then I got Eddie off to bed. Tina had made a point of telling me she had said her morning prayers today and I knew she had said her evening prayers before dinner. She stayed up for a while, talking about the tree problem, then excused herself.

"So it's up early tomorrow," Jack said.

"Yes, if you want to go to early mass."

"Sure, why not? We'll all drive over there together."

We made it an early night.

I woke up once during the night, thinking I heard something. I put on my robe and checked Eddie, who was sleeping soundly. I stopped at Tina's door, but there was no sound. I went back to bed.

We were both awakened a long time later by what sounded like a distant scream.

"What now?" Jack said irritably. He got out of bed, went to the window, and looked out. There was, of course, nothing to see, as our bedroom was tacked onto the back of the house. He left the room and came back a minute later. "Something doing down the street, near the Grosses'."

"Mel's house?" I scrambled out of bed and put on my robe. I went downstairs and opened the front door. Something was definitely happening down the block and as I stood there, I heard a siren.

"Can you tell what's going on?" Jack asked behind me. He had thrown on some clothes.

"There are some people standing in the street. That's all I can see. But they must have called the police or an ambulance."

"I heard the siren. I'll run down and see what's doing."

I went upstairs, listened at both closed doors, then put on a pair of jeans and a sweatshirt. The morning air was cool and I wanted to dash down and see what was happening for myself. Eddie would probably sleep another fifteen or twenty minutes and I wasn't going far.

I jogged down the block to where the Kovaks and Greiners had been shouting at each other a couple of days earlier. The small group had grown and the police car had arrived, then a second one. Jack turned and saw me.

"You don't want to look at this," he said.

"What is it?"

"Did you check Tina's room?"

"The door is closed. She's still asleep."

"She's dead, Chris."

"What?" I felt a wave of dizziness.

"I can't see the face, but it's her habit. It looks like she's been shot."

"I can't believe it. How—?"

"Go on back. Check her room. I'll stay here."

As I turned to go, two things struck me. Mel and Hal were coming out of their house, and the silver maple was lying across the Kovaks' driveway. Mel asked me what happened and I told her in breathless half sentences.

"Take it easy, Chris."

"She's my guest," I said. "She's staying at my house. How can this have happened?"

"Come on, I'll walk you back."

We went to my house and Mel came upstairs with me. I was shaking as I knocked at Tina's door, not believing she wasn't in there. When there was no answer, I opened the door. The bed was empty and unmade. Her duffle bag was on the desk chair, stuffed, ready to be zipped up.

"She's gone," I said.

"She left the door closed so you wouldn't know she had left her room."

"Maybe." I felt panicky. This could not have happened. My heart was racing and my mind was a jumble.

"Come on down, Chris. We'll have some coffee. Maybe Jack'll have some answers."

I let Mel make coffee while I sat thinking that this was all wrong. This was my home and I had lost all control. My guest was dead down the street, my friend was making coffee in my kitchen. I felt weak and powerless and confused.

Mel poured and I sipped from my cup. A moment later, I heard Eddie. It was one of those moments when I felt the weight of motherhood. It didn't matter whether you were sick or well, whether Tina was dead or alive, your child needed you and you went.

"I'll get him," Mel said.

"It's OK. I will."

I went upstairs, took him out of his crib, and held him close to me. The warmth of his body, the sweet smell of his skin, began to calm me. The panic began to drain.

"Go bekfast," Eddie said.

"Yes, let's go down to breakfast. Mel is here, Eddie."

"Mel," he said, the *l* coming out in something between a *y* and a *w*.

We got his breakfast together and I sat sipping my coffee and watching him until I heard the door open. I went to see Jack before he came into the kitchen.

"This is off the wall," he said.

"Is it Tina?"

"Looks like her to me."

"Oh, Jack."

He hugged me. "You gonna be OK?"

"Sure. Eddie's having breakfast. Mel's with him. What can you tell me?"

"Someone chopped down the tree between the Greiners and the Kovaks."

"I saw it."

"And somebody shot Tina."

"Do the police have Mr. Kovak's gun?"

"Afraid not. Kovak says it's been lost for months."

"What?"

"He says he reported it lost or stolen, but there's no record of the report. The cop radioed the station and they checked it."

"This is crazy. What was Tina doing there in the first place? Who would want to kill her? Why did she leave the house?"

"All good questions. Did you check her room?"

"The door was closed. Her duffle bag was already packed and ready to be zipped up. She left her bed unmade, as though she intended to come back. She's a neat girl. When I walked by her room yesterday, it looked like a convent room, everything in its place."

"The door was open when you went by?"

"Yes."

"So when she left in the middle of the night and closed the door, it was so you would think she was still there."

"I guess so."

"Let's not leave poor Mel alone with Eddie in the kitchen."

"Poor Mel" was coping exactly the way she always did, joking around with Eddie, who had by now finished his breakfast and drunk his milk. He ran to Jack who picked him up and talked to him. I looked at my watch and realized I didn't have to hurry for early mass. I wasn't going to St. Stephen's this morning.

I walked to the door with Mel, telling her what Jack had just told me.

"His gun is lost?" she said with disbelief.

"That's what he told the cop."

"I don't like this. I think there's a good chance that man shot Tina."

"But why? He didn't know her."

"She chopped down the tree."

"But Mel, he wanted the tree chopped down. And it's crazy to think that Tina would do that."

"You're right. It's the Greiners who loved the tree. My head isn't functioning very well this morning."

"Join the crowd. Maybe he chopped down the tree and Tina saw him do it."

"That makes sense. What do you think she was doing walking down the block early in the morning?"

"She's used to getting up early," I said. "Five o'clock is wake-up time at the convent. Maybe she got up, got dressed, and went outside to say her morning prayers. And then took a walk."

"And he was out there chopping down the tree and didn't want any witnesses."

"Did you hear a gunshot?"

"I don't know. I was sleeping till I heard the police siren. I could have heard a shot in my sleep and thought it was part of a dream."

"I hate this," I said. "I'm going to have to call St. Stephen's now and tell them. Mel, if Mr. Kovak is lying about losing the gun, he has to know he's a suspect. This girl was shot in front of his house and he's on record as owning a gun. The police can get a warrant and search his house. He really has to be irrational to think he can get away with this."

"Then maybe he didn't do it."

"But if he didn't—"

"I know. I have a feeling you're going to be spending a lot of time in the next few days thinking about this."

"And other things," I said, remembering Tina's story. "That poor girl."

Mel gave me a hug. "I've got a hungry family waiting for bagels and lox. I gotta go."

"Thanks for coming down."

"Keep me posted," she said, and off she went.

We had breakfast and then went off to mass. I hadn't called St. Stephen's yet but I wanted to do that when I came home from church. Church always put me in a calmer mood and when we got home there would be a day of questions and answers with the local police in addition to my call to the convent.

The police car was waiting at the curb and Officer Malcolm got out as we pulled into the drive. He came inside with us.

"We have no ID on the body," he said.

"I would appreciate it if we could not talk about this in front of my son," I said. "I haven't called the convent yet but I'm going to do that right now."

"Maybe you can get someone to come down and ID her."

"I'll do that."

"Oh, and happy Mother's Day, Mrs. Brooks."

I stared at him. It was Mother's Day. Tina had died on Mother's Day. "Thank you. I'll be back as soon as I can."

I left Eddie with Jack and went upstairs to our bedroom where I would not be overheard. Whoever's daughter Tina was, there would be no happy Mother's Days for the rest of her life. I dearly did not want to make this call. I sat on the edge of our bed looking at the phone, thinking of the anguish I was about to inflict on a whole string of individuals who had known, worked with, loved, and cared about Tina. Finally, I picked up the phone and dialed St. Stephen's.

The phone was not answered by Angela. It was Sunday and she had the day off. I didn't recognize the voice but I asked for Sister Joseph and she put me through without getting my name.

It took a few minutes for them to locate Joseph, but finally she picked up.

"This is Chris," I said.

"Chris. Are you all right? You don't sound your usual self."

"Joseph, I have something terrible to tell you."

"Has something happened to your family?" She sounded genuinely distressed.

"No, they're fine. It's a novice named Tina Richmond."

"Tina. She's gone home to visit her family. How do you come to know her?"

"She came here to Oakwood. She came to see me. Joseph, she's been murdered."

There were seconds of silence. I could imagine her trying to absorb what I had said as I had tried to only a couple of hours earlier. "Tina is dead?"

"Yes. She was shot. It happened down the block from us sometime early this morning. I'm not sure when. Joseph, I have to ask you or one of the other nuns to come down here and identify her."

"I'll come, of course." There was another short silence. She would be looking at the large round watch, figuring how long it would take her to get here, how soon she could leave, whether to take someone with her. "I'll leave in ten minutes. I'll be there as soon as I can."

"Joseph, if you'd like to stay overnight—you could bring a bag."

"I'll do that, just in case this takes a long time."

"I'm terribly sorry."

"I'll see you soon."

I hung up, feeling a little better and a little worse. I had gotten it over with. The phone call, at least, was behind me. But what was coming was a lot worse. I had no choice now. I had to talk to Joseph about Tina's birth and I would rather spend the next week in solitary confinement than do that.

I left our bedroom and went to the one Tina had stayed in. I knew the police would go through it very shortly and I wanted to take a look myself before they removed everything that Tina had brought.

The duffle bag was on the chair and I moved things around inside, looking for anything that wasn't clothing. I felt mostly soft fabric. There were secular clothes in there, toiletries, and a towel. I smoothed the clothes and left the bag as I had found it.

There was nothing on the bed, nothing left in the closet. She must have packed her nightgown before she left the house. I looked around and saw her black leather handbag on the night table. It was envelope style, a flap that folded over the top and latched with a clasp that went through a slot and then turned. The flap was closed, but the clasp hadn't been turned. I opened the bag and looked inside. There was a wallet with a few dollars in it, not enough, I thought, to pay for the train back to St. Stephen's, a Social Security card, and a telephone card with a number that I assumed made her calls home collect. There were two ballpoint pens, a little book for taking notes, and several clean tissues folded. I took out the notebook and opened it. Every page was blank. I dug to the bottom of the bag and felt a key ring. It had several keys on it, one that looked like a house key, one that was probably a car key, and a couple of others. There was a newspaper clipping with a picture of her parents, Anne and Herbert Richmond, at a charity dinner. They looked like pleasant people in their forties or so, and since I'm terrible at family resemblances, I saw none between them and their daughter.

Aside from those few things, I found a paper clip and a couple of safety pins. I put them all back, replaced the flap as I had found it, and went downstairs to get things started.

8

"Which of you would like to go first?" Officer Malcolm asked when I joined them.

"Why don't you, Chris? I'll take Eddie outside. You spent a lot more time with Tina than I did."

That was certainly true. I waited till he and Eddie had gone out, then turned to the young man in uniform. "What would you like to know?" I asked.

"I'd like to get your recollections while they're still fresh. A detective may come by later but I want to know when you last saw the deceased."

"Last night," I said. "We all had dinner together and she went upstairs before we did."

"Did you hear anything during the night?"

"I thought I did. I got out of bed, checked my son, and saw that Tina's door was closed. I didn't look inside. The door was still closed this morning when they found her body."

"So she could have left at any time."

"Yes."

"Is she a friend of yours? A relative?"

"I never saw her before Thursday when she turned up on my doorstep."

59

"Can you tell me about that?"

I told him of my connection to St. Stephen's and of Tina's. I didn't say a word about Joseph or about Tina's crazy story.

"Did she tell you why she wanted to see you?"

"She was having problems. She'd heard of me and I guess she found my address at the convent. She wanted to talk to me and find some resolution for her troubles."

"What were these problems, Mrs. Brooks?"

I took a deep breath. It was rare that I was on this end of an interview in a homicide. When I asked questions, I expected to be given answers, complete answers. Now I was the one holding back and I knew he would not be happy. "They were very personal. I really can't talk about them. I'm sorry."

"We need to know as much as possible to find the killer," he said calmly.

"I know you do, and I'll help you in any way I can. But she described something that is little more than a fantasy and it involves other people. I can't discuss it."

"Do you happen to know where we can find her family?"

I felt relieved that he didn't press me. Probably when they brought the detectives in, I'd have a harder time, but for the moment we were moving on to simpler questions. "I do. Tina gave me the names and address of her parents. I'll get it for you." I got up and found my notebook.

He copied from it into his. "Have you spoken to them?"

"No. I called the Superior at St. Stephen's, the convent where Tina was a novice. She's on her way down here now to identify the body."

"Any idea how long it'll take for her to get here?"

"Less than two hours. Do you know where they've taken Tina?"

"To the local hospital. We can drive over when the Superior comes."

"OK."

"So you don't really know anything about this girl."

"Very little. She rang my doorbell and introduced herself. I told her she could stay a few days, but no longer than that. She said she'd go back to the convent today."

"You have any idea why she might have been out early in the morning?"

I told him what I had told Mel, that she might have said her morning prayers outside and then gone for a walk. "Do you have any idea how long she was dead before she was found?" I asked.

"No idea at all."

Not that he would have told me if he did know. "I don't know what else I can tell you. She left her bed unmade so I assume she intended to come back and make it. We were going to go to early mass this morning and then I was going to drive her back to the convent."

"That's a long trip for you, almost two hours each way."

"By train it's longer and you have to change. I didn't mind and she was happy that I offered."

"I guess that's it. I'd appreciate it if you'd leave her room as she left it. The crime-scene detectives will want to have a look at it. If you decide to tell us anything else, you know where to find us."

We went outside together and Jack and I traded places. I was sure the officer wanted to make certain we didn't exchange any remarks. I didn't think Jack would tell him about the Joseph story, which was the only thing I cared about. I took Eddie back inside and upstairs to change his clothes into something he could run around in. We had just come home from church and weren't wearing our running-around clothes.

Officer Malcolm didn't spend much time with Jack, either. By the time Eddie and I had changed and were out back, Jack joined us. I heard the police car leave a moment later.

"I refused to tell him what Tina's problem was," I said, not asking.

"I told him anything I knew was secondhand and if he didn't get it from you, I didn't think I should say anything."

"Thanks."

"Is Sister Joseph coming?"

"She's on her way. I suggested she bring an overnight bag in case she wants to stay. The only problem is, she'd have to stay in the room Tina used."

"I'll get her a room at the motel. She won't mind that, will she?"

"I don't think so. Officer Malcolm," I added, "said a detective would probably question us."

"I'm sure they'll dig one up, maybe from the county. Are you going to tell Sister Joseph what Tina said?"

"I think I have to. It could be connected with her death."

"Not if Kovak did it."

"There's so much going on here, Jack. How is it possible for a man to become so enraged over a tree that he would murder a girl who saw him cut it down?"

"Mr. Brooks?"

We turned around. Coming toward us from the driveway was another Oakwood police officer.

"I'm Jack Brooks. Something up?"

"Do you folks have an ax?"

"I think so. It's in the garage. Why?"

"I'd like to see it, if you don't mind."

"No trouble."

I checked Eddie, who was sitting on the patio and playing with toys. Then I followed them to the garage.

"You know where the ax is, Chris?"

"Along the right-hand wall somewhere. It should be hanging so that Eddie can't reach it."

"I don't see it."

I felt myself becoming impatient. What did this policeman want with our ax and why couldn't Jack just find it? I walked in alongside my car and looked up. We had other tools hanging from hooks that Jack had installed after Eddie was born and we became more careful, a spade, a hoe, a rake, a leaf rake, even a pitchfork, which I had teased him made him look like a Russian peasant at work. I couldn't find the ax.

"Any reason you're looking for it?" Jack asked the officer.

"Mr. Kovak's ax is in his garage and so is the Greiners'. We're trying to find out where the ax that cut down the tree came from."

"Well, it didn't come from here," Jack said, and I could hear irritation in his voice.

"But you own one?"

"Yes, we own one. I had to cut down some small trees last summer and I bought one. It should be right here."

"On that empty hook?"

"Yeah, on that empty hook."

"If you find it, will you give me a call?"

"I'll do that," Jack said. He wasn't using his friendly, suburban homeowner voice. He was sounding more like a put-upon New York cop.

"This is not possible."

We looked at each other, both of us too confused and surprised to know what else to say. "Was the garage door locked last night?" I asked.

"I don't know. You don't know either, I can tell."

He was right. Although Jack is very security conscious, we weren't very careful about locking the garage. Our garage is not attached to the house so it's not a way inside. It's very old, the lock might qualify as an antique, and we frequently have trouble locking and unlocking it. Usually, I park my car inside and Jack parks his just outside the garage door. The only things inside that can be stolen are garden tools and a couple of Eddie's outdoor toys. So we don't worry about it very much.

"You know what he's driving at, don't you?" Jack said.

"I don't want to think about it."

"Did you see the ax that was used to cut down the tree?"

"I saw it lying there but I didn't go over to look at it."

"You think it was ours?"

"Jack, it was an ax. It had a long handle and an ax blade. I'm not an expert on tools. I have no idea who the manufacturer of our ax is. I'm just starting to feel that we're in the middle of something terrible."

"That's an understatement." He looked as angry as I had ever seen him. "I'm going in and changing. Let's get Eddie fed and off to his nap so we can go through the garage. Maybe I put the damn thing somewhere else, like the basement. I wish I could remember the last time I used it."

We went inside and I got Eddie's lunch started. While I was setting things out, the front doorbell rang. What now? I thought as I went to answer it.

"Flowers for Mrs. Brooks," the young man holding a large box said.

"Oh." Everything inside me melted. I forgot the missing ax, poor Tina, Joseph on her way to make a terrible identification. My husband had sent me flowers and as always happened, I felt teary.

"Enjoy them," the young man called as he went back to the van parked in front of our house.

I opened the box in the living room and found a dozen yellow roses and a small card. I told Eddie I'd be right back and I carried it all upstairs to our bedroom. Jack was pulling a sweatshirt over his head when I walked in. As he looked at me, he smiled.

"Thank you," I said, feeling tears tumble down my cheeks.

He took the box, put it on the bed, and put his arms around me. "Best mommy in the world," he said.

"Thank you." I kissed his neck. "Thank you, thank you."

"Let me put my sneakers on and I'll be right down."

"They're just beautiful." I kissed him again and went downstairs.

Joseph arrived soon after Eddie had gone to sleep. Jack was out back looking for our missing ax and I was starting to think of this as a sick comedy rather than a tragedy, until I looked at Joseph's face. She looked awful.

"This is not the kind of news I have ever gotten before," she said when she was sitting in our family room. "I haven't called Tina's parents yet. I thought I'd like to see her first."

"Sure. Let's have a light lunch and then I'll call the police. They'll drive us over."

"You don't have to come, Chris."

"Yes, I do."

She looked at the vase with the yellow roses. "It's Mother's Day, isn't it?" She smiled. "And someone remembered you."

"Yes. He's very good at remembering. He'll be in in a minute."

The door closed just about then and Jack came in. He's very formal with Joseph, very respectful. They shook hands and he asked if she had had a good ride up. Then we sat down to our lunch.

"I hope you'll stay overnight, Sister Joseph," Jack said. "I've made a reservation for you at our local motel and I'm cooking dinner for us."

"Let me see how the afternoon goes, Jack. Thank you very much."

As soon as we were done, I called Officer Malcolm and he came over. I introduced him to Joseph and he apologized to have taken her away from her work.

"We have a detective on his way right now. He'll be coming over to look at the room Miss Richmond slept in and to talk to you." He said this to Jack who replied that it was fine; he had no plans to go anywhere at the moment.

We went out and sat in the back of the police car.

Officer Malcolm assured us this would take very little time.

"Have you notified her parents yet?" I asked him.

"No, ma'am. I'd like her identified before we make the call."

"I'll call them," Joseph said. "I think that would be much better than their hearing it from a police officer."

He said nothing else for the rest of the drive, which took only ten minutes. I didn't tell Joseph what I wanted to discuss with her, deciding that could wait till we were back at the house with no strangers present.

"I'll drop off you ladies and park the car," Officer Malcolm said as he entered the hospital complex.

"We'll be glad to walk," Joseph said, but he swung around the front of the building and stopped at the main entrance.

"Won't take a minute." I closed the door and he drove off.

"Thank you for coming, Chris. This is a terrible thing to have to do."

"I wouldn't have let you come alone. And besides, I want to make sure this is the person who stayed with us for the last few days. I didn't see her face this morning."

Officer Malcolm returned and led us through the hospital as though he knew the way, which surprised me. There weren't many mysterious deaths in the Oakwood area.

I knew this hospital myself because until a few years ago my cousin's home for retarded adults was housed in a wing and I visited him there frequently. I had even had an experience in the basement, where we were now headed, that I would be happy to forget.

"They know we're coming," Officer Malcolm said. "They've got her ready." We were standing in front of a door that said MORGUE and I was feeling very jittery. "You ladies OK?"

We nodded and he opened the door. Inside there were two pallets with covered bodies on them. A woman in scrubs was sitting at a desk and turned when we entered.

"Officer Malcolm?" she said.

"Yes, ma'am. This is Mrs. Brooks and Sister Joseph."

"I'm Dr. Kenworthy. You're here to see the girl who was shot this morning?"

"Yes," we both said.

"I'm sorry we're not set up with TV cameras to make it easy on you. I'll draw the sheet back and you can see her face."

We walked closer and Dr. Kenworthy turned down the sheet.

"That's Tina," I said, feeling the horror of seeing a young person lying stiff and without color.

Joseph moved a little closer. She took her glasses off and rubbed them on her habit, her eyes never moving from the still face. She put her glasses back on and stood for another moment. Then she shook her head. "I've never seen her before," she said.

"That's not Tina?" I asked.

"No. She's about Tina's age, but Tina doesn't look anything like that."

"Would you like to walk around and look at her from the side?" the doctor said.

"No. I'm sure. That's not Tina Richmond." She turned away from the body and I could see the distress in her face.

"Thanks, Doctor," Officer Malcolm said.

The doctor looked startled. She stood beside the girl's body and watched as we left the room.

9

There was a police car outside our house when we got back. Officer Malcolm thanked us and dropped us off on the driveway.

"I thought for a moment I just wasn't recognizing her," Joseph said as we walked toward the front door. "But that's not Tina. I've never seen that girl before and she looks nothing like Tina. I'll call her home when I get back to St. Stephen's and make sure everything's all right."

"Joseph, I'd like you to stay overnight. I would have given you our guest room but it's where Tina—or whoever she is—stayed and the police asked us not to touch it till they've had a chance to look at it. Jack and I are paying for your motel room and I think you'll be very comfortable there. There are some things we should talk about."

She looked at her watch. "If you think it's important, I'll stay."

"I do. You can call St. Stephen's and tell them. And call the Richmonds also. It looks like the detective is here, so I'll have to answer more questions. Let's go inside."

The detective was upstairs looking at Tina's room. Jack came down and I told him what had happened.

"This is weird. Is Sister Joseph staying over?"

"Yes. I told her I wanted to talk to her."

"I'll be going out in a while to get the makings of dinner so you two can be alone. Does she have any idea who this girl was?"

"None."

"Well, they're taking prints off the ax they found. I think it's ours. They think it's ours, too. Who the hell can that girl have been?"

"She was carrying Tina's ID. I looked in the room before I was told not to. Tina's Social Security card is in her bag."

"I hope the real Tina is alive and well."

"Joseph is checking on that now."

It turned out to be rather a longer conversation than I had anticipated and before Joseph was off the phone, the detective came downstairs.

"You must be Mrs. Brooks," he said affably. "I'm Detective Joe Fox. Sorry it took me so long to get here but they couldn't find me."

"That's OK." I offered my hand and we shook.

"Can we sit somewhere and have a little chat?"

"Let's try the dining room," I said.

We sat down at the table, which I used more for arranging my notes than for eating, and he took out his notebook and pen.

"Have you heard about the identification of the body?" I asked.

"Not yet. That's where you just came from, right?"

"The dead girl is definitely the one who stayed here

for the last three nights, but Sister Joseph, the Superior of St. Stephen's Convent, says it isn't Tina Richmond."

"Well, that's a nice turn of events. I take it she's here for me to talk to."

"She's on the phone now, talking to the real Tina Richmond's parents."

"Who live in New Jersey," he said, looking at a page in his book.

"That's right."

"Well, I'll be talking to her when you and I get finished."

He went through everything Officer Malcolm had gone through and then said, "Wayne Malcolm tells me this young lady had some kind of problem that you refused to talk about."

"Detective, at this point, having found out that the girl I thought was Tina isn't even Tina, I don't think I should talk about something that involves other people and was probably a total fantasy anyway. And if there's any truth to it, does it involve the real Tina or this poor dead girl?"

He looked at his notebook, which lay in front of him on the table, and frowned. "I see your point, but the story might help us find out who this 'poor dead girl' is."

"I don't think so. I think it may just hurt the reputation of people who have nothing whatever to do with this girl." I was trying to be as vague as possible. I certainly didn't want him to suspect that Sister Joseph was the person I was protecting.

"I've talked to your husband," he said. "He won't say anything about it either."

"What he knows he heard from me. He's not a primary source."

"I'll let you go on this for the time being. But if I have to come back, I promise you I won't be Mr. Nice Guy the second time around."

"Fair enough."

"Let's see if Sister Joseph is off the phone."

He came with me into the kitchen. The phone was on the counter and Joseph wasn't there. We went into the family room and Joseph stood up as she saw us.

"I'm Sister Joseph," she said.

"Detective Joe Fox. Would you like to come with me, Sister?"

I went outside and found Jack still rummaging through the garage.

"You done?"

"For the time being. He's in the dining room with Joseph. You want to run your errand now so we won't all starve?"

He gave me a grin. "I'm on my way. And I promise you, nobody will starve."

The detective left about fifteen minutes later. He said he was finished with the bedroom upstairs, that he had removed everything he needed from the room. Joseph offered to stay there, to save us the expense of the motel, but I felt she would be more comfortable by herself.

I knew Eddie would be up soon and I wanted to get as much of our conversation out of the way as possible before he joined us. We sat in the family room and I asked about her phone call to the Richmonds.

"Tina is there—I talked to her—and she has no idea who would be masquerading as her. She said one thing that was interesting. A few weeks ago she lost her pocket-book. It contained her wallet with a small amount of money, and some identification. She said her Social Security card was there. She thought she might receive the wallet back, minus the money—that often happens, you know; the thief throws away the bag after he's robbed it—but it never came back, and just this week she applied for a replacement."

"Where did this happen?"

"She said it was on a day that she was taking classes at the college."

"So another student might have walked off with it."

"That's right. But she has no idea who that could be, or even if it was a student. She said she was carrying books so she didn't notice it wasn't on her arm."

I knew exactly what she meant. When Eddie was born, I had to carry so many things, I found that occasionally I left my bag behind because other weights took its place on my arm. "The body that we saw a little while ago, you're sure that wasn't a student at the college?"

"I'm not sure. I know I said I'd never seen her before, but I really meant that wasn't Tina. I couldn't swear I've never seen that girl. But she isn't a novice at St. Stephen's."

"Do you usually know all the students?"

"I do usually recognize them. This is very difficult. I've been thinking about that poor child, wondering if she might be a student, if she might be someone from town who drops in and listens to lectures. That happens, you know."

"Someone will report her missing," I said.

"When she came to you she was dressed in our novice's habit?"

"Yes. I recognized it immediately when I opened the door. And Tina's Social Security card was in her handbag. And a newspaper clipping of Tina's parents with their picture."

"So there was enough information that this young imposter could have posed as Tina."

"Where did she get the habit from?"

"I suppose it's not all that difficult to snatch one from the laundry."

"You know," I said, thinking about the days that Tina was here, "I suggested to her that she say her morning and evening prayers. The first morning, she woke up fairly late. In fact, I went upstairs after Jack left and rousted her."

"So she might not have been on a nun's schedule."

"Yesterday she made a point of telling me she had said her prayers." I opened my notebook. "Joseph, I have to tell you what this girl, whoever she is, said was a problem in her life. It involves you and this is the hardest thing I've ever had to talk to you about."

"Go on." She looked her usual implacable self. If she had any idea of what was coming, I certainly could not see any traces.

"This girl, I'll call her Tina, told me that she was your natural child." I had decided to say it as briefly as I could. The details, if Joseph wanted them, would come later.

"That's quite an accusation," she said.

"I want you to know, before you say anything else, I have not discussed this with the police. Neither has Jack."

"Thank you. When is this birth supposed to have happened?"

"She said she was twenty."

"Twenty years ago. Yes, that's very convenient. I wasn't at St. Stephen's twenty years ago."

"I see." I didn't know where to go from there. Of course, I wanted answers because in the answers might be something that would lead us to the killer of the girl who was still nameless. But I didn't want Joseph to feel that she owed me an explanation of where she was and what she was doing twenty years ago. "If you don't want to talk about it," I said, "I'll—"

"I think we must talk about it. There's a dead girl in the hospital morgue, a girl who came to you and might still be alive if she hadn't. She's not likely to have fingerprints on record anywhere. I don't suppose at her age she joined the army or the FBI. So finding out who she is and why she's dead and who might have killed her aren't going to be easy."

"But your life is your business. When she told me this wild tale, I thought it was just that, a wild tale. I was hesitant about letting her stay here because I thought she might be psychotic, but she acted fairly normal. Until this morning. It appears that she took our ax out of the garage and chopped down a tree down the block and across the street, a tree that's been the subject of a lot of neighborhood dissension."

"Yes, my life is my business. As yours is yours. I don't look forward to seeing it displayed publicly and talked about by strangers. Where did this girl say she was born?"

I turned a page in my notebook. "At Good Samaritan Hospital in some town in Ohio. I have it here somewhere."

"I know the hospital," Joseph said. "I was a patient there once."

I felt a cold shudder. "She said—" I swallowed. "She said she was adopted through God's Love adoption agency."

"But what we don't know is whether this girl was speaking for Tina or speaking for her real self. And that's crucial."

"I agree. It would be easy enough to find out if Tina was adopted."

"And what agency handled the adoption. Shall we start there?"

"Let's."

Joseph went to the kitchen and made the call. While she was talking, I heard Eddie talking to himself upstairs. I went up, got him out of his crib, and brought him down. I got a glass of milk and a couple of pretzels and took him to the family room to eat and drink. Joseph got off the phone just as he was getting started.

They made some conversation and Eddie offered her one of his pretzels, an act of generosity that surprised me. She assured him she wasn't hungry and he went back to his snack.

When he was finished, we went outside, taking two summer chairs to the sandbox so we could continue our conversation.

"Tina is their natural child," Joseph said, "the third of five children. She was born in New Jersey."

"Then our nameless stranger was talking about herself, not about Tina."

"Tina?" Eddie said.

"Tina's gone home, Eddie."

"OK," he said. "Bye-bye."

Joseph smiled as she watched him. "You do have to be careful, don't you?"

"Very."

"Well, why don't we refer to your mysterious visitor as Anita? That's the other name spelled backwards with an extra *a*."

"Good idea." I moved my chair a little distance away from the sandbox. "Joseph, what would motivate this stranger to concoct a story like the one she told me?"

"I can't imagine. It's hard to blackmail a nun who doesn't have a great deal of money to pay. And what could she have wanted from you? You and Jack would never pay her."

"None of that is clear. She said she lived in fear of you, that you had realized the relationship between you and that you might do something terrible to her."

"That's preposterous, don't you think? I never met her. And if what she said was true, would she think I might hurt my own child?"

"If your position was threatened."

"She certainly doesn't sound very stable."

"Joseph, I told the police that Anita had a problem but I refused to tell them what it was. Now that I have your denial, if they come back and ask again, I'll tell them I have nothing to say."

"I certainly appreciate that, but I don't want you spending a night in jail on my behalf."

"It would complicate my life, no doubt about it," I said lightly. "Do you want me to continue to look into this?"

"I think we have a duty to try to find Anita's killer. Whoever she is, whatever stories she's told, she didn't deserve what happened to her."

10

Jack came home a little while later and told us in no uncertain terms that he was busy in the kitchen and not to be disturbed. He carried in two bags of groceries from our fancier supermarket, more food than I could imagine all of us eating twice over. Eddie wanted to see what Daddy was doing so I took him inside for a minute to watch Jack putting things in the refrigerator—and hiding them from me as he did so.

"No fair opening this," he ordered.

"Yes, sir. I think we'll take a walk and keep out of your way."

"Sounds like a good idea."

The rest of us set off for the nearby beach. Oakwood is on the Long Island Sound and a group of home-owners, including us, own a private beach on a quiet cove. It was still too cool to consider a dip, but it was always a nice place to walk and Eddie loved the sand.

The sun was shining when we got there and the air was warm and breezy. Eddie sat down in the sand and started to pull off his shoes.

"He certainly knows what he wants," Joseph said.

"He sure does." I took the shoes and socks and let him frolic.

"I think I should fill you in on some of my life, Chris, so that you can see the connections and lack of connections between me and the story this young woman told."

"Joseph, I don't want you to tell me anything that you would prefer to keep to yourself."

"There have been many things in my life that I wanted to keep to myself when I was younger and some that I still wish to keep private. But it's not a secret that I grew up in a wonderful family with parents who loved me, two sisters that I am close to, and a brother that I haven't seen for some time. We lived outside of Cincinnati and I went to school not far from my home. I came to St. Stephen's through the college when I was eighteen and looking for an education that I could afford and that my family would accept. I never left St. Stephen's after I registered as a freshman."

"So your life was divided between Ohio and New York."

"That's right. At this point, I'm much more of a New Yorker than an Ohioan. About twenty or twenty-one years ago, I asked for leave to go home. There were problems in my family that I thought I might be able to help solve. I was given indefinite leave and I went back. I thought I would be there a few months, but it worked out to be much longer than that. Since I'm not a person who can sit and twiddle her thumbs, I got a job as soon as I could and started working several days a week."

"Did you wear your habit?"

"Interesting that you ask. I had intended to, but the office manager said it might make some of the employees uncomfortable. I received permission from St. Stephen's to wear street clothes. I must tell you," she smiled at the recollection, "it was a time of miniskirts and shorts and

I had a terrible time finding skirts and dresses that I considered appropriate. One of my sisters, who is a talented seamstress, quickly ran up a few dark skirts and I bought several blouses to go with them. I didn't want to rush around with my knees showing."

I smiled. I couldn't imagine Joseph in a short skirt. I find I myself can hardly wear anything comfortably if it doesn't cover my knees. "So you were able to keep your job."

"Oh, yes, and I enjoyed it. I was used to turning in my paycheck to the convent, so I just turned it in to my family instead. It was an interesting year—I must have been there close to a year—and when I felt I had done what I set out to do, I went back to St. Stephen's. I remember that I laid all those nice skirts and blouses on my bed for whoever wanted them and I put my habit back on. I felt like a different person. I was very grateful for the opportunity to hold a secular job, have secular friends, live fairly independently, enjoy myself, and really want to get back to my calling."

"Did you have anything to do with God's Love adoption agency?"

"Not that I remember. I worked for an insurance agency doing mostly clerical work, although later they had me do more demanding things like make inquiries and conduct interviews. If that adoption agency had business that crossed my desk, it was just one of many hundreds and I don't recall the name specifically."

"You said you were once a patient at the same Good Samaritan Hospital that Anita claimed to have been born in. Was it during that year?"

"No, it wasn't. I broke my arm when I was a child and I was taken there to have it set. There were some complications, I think, and they kept me overnight. But I must tell you, I visited someone at that hospital during the year I spent in Ohio."

"But there would be no record of that."

"I wouldn't think so."

"Anita said that the adoption was handled by a woman named Mrs. DelBello. Does that name ring a bell?"

"I can't say it does. I've met a lot of people in my life and one of them may have been named DelBello, but as far as that particular year, I don't think so."

"You said you visited someone in Good Samaritan Hospital the year of your leave."

"That's right. It was a cousin I was fond of."

"Was it one visit or several?"

She seemed to wait a moment before answering. "It was a number of times, Chris, many, many times. He was a man I cared a great deal for and he was very ill. He died during that year." She looked away, at the sand, at Eddie, at the water washing the beach. "At that time, the hospice movement wasn't as developed as it is now. He was too sick to be cared for at home but there was nowhere else for him to go except a hospital."

"Did he have family?" I asked.

"A child, a son. He was quite young."

She didn't mention a wife and I didn't pursue it. "He must have been a fairly young man," I said, thinking that twenty years ago she herself was not yet thirty.

"He was, yes. He lived a greatly shortened life. It's one of those tragedies for which we can never know the reason, one that tested my faith."

It was clear that this death still affected her and I was sorry I had asked her the initial question, sorry I had caused the pain she was obviously suffering.

"On those visits," I said, "could you have talked to someone in a waiting room and disclosed who you were, someone who might have somehow used your identity to hurt you?"

"I don't remember waiting rooms, Chris. I generally went to the hospital after work or on weekends and I went directly to my cousin's room. I don't talk much about myself and I have no recollection of unburdening myself to any strangers that I met in the hospital. My cousin, of course, knew all about me, but that's not what you're after."

"Joseph, I think the first thing we have to do is find out who Anita was, where she really comes from, what her connection to St. Stephen's was, and then maybe we'll know why she told me this monstrous story. I'm going to ask the Oakwood police to get me a picture of her. I hate the idea of showing a picture of a dead girl around, but someone around the convent must have seen her if she had a novice's habit. Perhaps the real Tina will know who she is. Maybe they shared a class and became friends. Somehow or other Anita learned about me."

"We do talk about you, you know," Joseph said with a smile. "You're one of our favorite people."

"Is my name and address in a file somewhere?"

"I'm sure it's in Angela's file. Angela keeps records of everyone. It's the most comprehensive one we have. And of course, you're in my personal file, too, along with Jack's name and Eddie's. Once I learn them, they're with me forever but when I first hear them, I write them down to be sure I don't make a mistake. But my file is in my office and it's off-limits to anyone except me."

I looked at my watch. We had been talking for quite

some time and standing on the beach long enough that I was getting anxious to be on the move. Suddenly, there was a cry of agony from Eddie. I looked around and saw him crying and spitting.

"Eddie, what's the matter?"

"No good," he said. "No good." He had put a handful of sand in his mouth and now was trying to rid himself of it.

"Oh, you poor thing," I said consolingly. I reached into my pocket and found a tissue. "Here, let me see if I can get it off your tongue."

He stood obediently still, tears lining his face, as I cleaned away the grains of sand. "Is that better?"

"Pooey," he said, and Joseph laughed.

"Pooey it is," I said. "Why don't we walk home and we'll get some water?"

He pointed to the sound. "Water."

"I'm afraid that's salty water, Eddie. You can't drink it."

"I want water."

"You'll get water, but not that water."

He started to cry again as we left the beach.

"There's something new to learn every day, isn't there?" Joseph said. "For you as well as for him."

"And some of them are hard lessons. For me, too. I should have watched him more closely."

"Don't blame yourself. You're a fine mother, Chris. I really mean that."

We talked less on the way back to the house, partly because I was thinking about all the things I would have to explore to come up with answers, partly because Eddie was still unhappy that there were grains of sand left in his mouth. Jack was cooking up a storm in the kitchen so we took a detour and went in through the front door, to avoid going through his domain. After a good rinse, Eddie eventually got back to his normally happy outlook and before he showed signs of evening hunger and fatigue, Jack fired up the barbecue.

It turned out to be an extraordinary dinner. He had bought a filet mignon, the kind of expense I could never have justified to myself—as he well knew—and he served it with an array of unusual mushrooms that he had cooked in a cast-iron pan. There were fresh vegetables as well, and a wonderful crusty bread with olives that he warmed up before serving.

Dessert was a died-and-gone-to-heaven cake from a bakery I try to stay away from. Before we ate it, I got Eddie off to bed. He would get a small piece tomorrow.

Joseph was generous in her praise. "I can't remember the last time I ate filet mignon, Jack. That is truly a gift."

"Nor I," I said.

"That's why I made it. Chris would never order it in a restaurant because it's the most expensive thing on the menu, and I wanted her to have it and enjoy it."

"Well, although it's hard to say on a day like this, it's my good fortune to be able to share it."

A little while later I drove to the motel, with Joseph following in her car.

I had a few more questions I wanted to ask Joseph before I left but we were hardly in her room when the phone rang. She answered and I heard her address Detective Fox.

"Yes, if you come right away," she said. "That's fine. I'll meet you in the lobby."

"He's coming to question you again?" I said when she hung up.

"It looks that way. Let me just freshen up and we'll go downstairs and wait for him."

I knew she would not care to be questioned by him alone in her room and it was doubtful whether he would allow me to be present. Five minutes later we had found in the lobby a sofa and chairs with a table in front of them, and as we sat down Detective Fox came in the front door, spotted us, and joined us.

I went as far from them as I could manage and sat on a chair with my back to them. I'm one of those people who never learned to sit quietly and do nothing. If only I had brought a book with me, I thought, but I had expected to talk to Joseph for a little while and then drive home. So I pulled out my notebook and tried to make sense of what had happened since I opened the door on Thursday and saw on my doorstep a young woman wearing the habit of a Franciscan novice.

But there was no sense. There were apparent coincidences that were explainable. If Joseph hadn't been in Ohio twenty years ago, there would be no case for her being the natural mother of a girl born in that part of the state. But I was satisfied with Joseph's explanation. She was there but she had not given birth to anyone then or ever. How this girl that we called Anita had come upon her name was the mystery we had to solve.

But even that wouldn't tell us why Anita had been murdered or by whom. Perhaps it was simply what it appeared to be, an act of violence against a tree that irrationally provoked a killing. Why on earth would Anita take our ax out of our garage and chop down that tree? And if she hadn't, who had? Jack's fingerprints would be all over it but I didn't think anyone would come and arrest him for either killing the tree or killing Anita.

I shut my notebook and twisted around to see how they were doing. Joseph was talking, her head bent. I hated having to intrude on her life with my questions, but where would I be without her answers?

A woman with a small dog sat down in the chair next to me and started a conversation. I participated half-heartedly until Detective Fox appeared in front of me.

"Want to change places, Mrs. Brooks?"

I was tempted to say "gladly," but I didn't. I excused myself from the lady and the dog, and sat down with Detective Fox.

"Sister Joseph will be waiting for you in her room," he began. "She told me what the girl who called herself Tina Richmond told you, that she was the sister's illegitimate child."

"She told you that?"

"Yes, she did, and she denied the truth of the accusation. She couldn't give me any more information because she said you were the one who got it firsthand from the girl."

"I was."

"OK, then." He flipped a page. "Let's do it."

I told him what I knew, mentioning the hospital, the adoption agency, and Mrs. DelBello. I assured him I had no idea who the dead girl was. During the brief period that I knew her, I had been convinced she was Tina Richmond.

We finished fairly quickly and I asked him if he could give me a picture of the dead girl. He asked what I wanted it for.

"Someone at or near St. Stephen's must have seen her," I said. "I'd like to see if someone recognizes her face."

"We'll be looking into that ourselves."

"Sister Joseph and I may think of people that don't occur to you."

He stared at me, kind of sizing me up. Then he reached into a pocket and pulled out a small snapshot. "If you find a connection, I hope you'll share it with me."

"I will."

He handed me the picture and I looked at it, a chill running through me. It was surely the face we had seen this afternoon, cold and pale and unmoving, but I wondered if it would be recognized by people who had known her when she was warm and filled with color and life.

"Not pretty," he said.

"Do you know yet if she was shot with Mr. Kovak's gun?"

"Not yet. The autopsy's tomorrow. I only got these pictures because I made a special request."

Two minutes later I was knocking on Joseph's door.

"I didn't expect you to tell him," I said to her.

"Chris, I really couldn't let you put yourself in a position of withholding information."

"I told him what Anita told me. There's nothing else. He gave me this." I showed her the picture.

"Will you come up to St. Stephen's yourself or shall I show it around?"

"I'll come up tomorrow. I'll bring Eddie."

"He'll get plenty of attention."

"Joseph, this is very awkward. I don't know your name. If I'm going to look into this, I'll need it."

"I was christened Katherine Marie. My family name is Bailey. Both my parents are dead. I have two sisters who are married and still live in Ohio and a brother who is somewhere on God's earth, but we don't know where. His name is Timothy." She took the little notepad by the side of the telephone and wrote on it. "Here are my sisters' names and addresses and the address where I grew up."

"What about the insurance company you worked for the year of your leave?"

She wrote on a second sheet. "Anything else?"

There was something else but I didn't want to ask. "I think that's it."

"I'll give you the name of my cousin's son, too," she said.

I took the small pieces of paper and put them in my bag without looking at them. "I'll see you tomorrow."

"Happy Mother's Day," Joseph said.

11

Jack and I talked about it, of course. I mentioned that I had thought he might stand beside me as my attorney when I was questioned and he admitted he had thought about it, but decided there was no reason to and doing so would just have antagonized the police. It really wasn't until after we had both been questioned the first time that the issue of the ax had come up.

"You think it's ours, don't you?" I asked.

"I'm sure of it. Ours is missing. What the hell was that girl thinking?"

"Mel and I talked about the tree with her yesterday. She seemed very distressed that people would fight over something so inconsequential. I think maybe she decided to take care of it her own way. She could have chopped it down, put the ax back in the garage, and gone back to bed before we were up."

"It sounds crazy, but I told you, she struck me as not very stable."

I had showed him the picture. "I'm taking Eddie up to St. Stephen's tomorrow to try to see if anyone up there recognizes that girl."

"Better be careful. I wouldn't be surprised if the Oakwood cops take a trip up there themselves. They have to start somewhere and that's about the only place to begin."

"I'm really troubled by the coincidence of this girl being born in that hospital during a time when Joseph was in the area."

"You don't really think—"

"I don't. But she visited that hospital. She was there a lot. She may never have been on the floor where new mothers are, but she went up and down in elevators with people who did visit that floor. There's a connection somehow. I have to try to find that Mrs. DelBello and see if she remembers handling an adoption that year from that hospital."

"Go to it."

"That was a great dinner, Jack."

He gave me a grin and leaned over and kissed me. "Suitable for a great mommy. Not to mention a great wife."

"Wow. I'm starting to feel victim to the sin of pride."

"You deserve it. For myself, it's lust I have to watch out for. You look very sexy right now."

I gave him a hug. "Yellow roses, filet mignon, chocolate cake to die for, and now he says I look sexy. You must be looking for a nomination for perfect husband of the year."

"Too many contenders. Let's go up and work off all those calories."

Eddie and I drove up to St. Stephen's the next morning. Angela knew I was coming and ran out to greet us, as always the first happy face we saw on our arrival. This time Eddie remembered her and went off happily without me.

Before that, I showed the picture to Angela, who already knew what had happened in Oakwood.

"I don't know, Chris," she said, holding the picture in front of her and looking at it from different perspectives. "I don't think I've ever seen her, but I could be wrong. I sit in that little telephone room and people pass and I just don't see them."

"Well, I'm going to ask around. Have fun, you two."

I watched them toddle off, Eddie hanging on to Angela's finger. Then I went around the outside of the Mother House and entered through the kitchen.

While many of the nuns enjoyed cooking and got the chance to do so on weekends or special occasions, most of the serious cooking was done by a paid staff, a cook and her helper. They also did the clean-up so they were busy many hours of the day. It was a little after eleven when I stepped into their domain. The cook knew me, but her young assistant was new in the last year or so and we hadn't met.

I explained that I was going to show them a picture of an unidentified young woman who was dead and who might have been around the St. Stephen's kitchen. When they agreed to look at it, I set it on the large wooden counter that they used to prepare the food. I ran my fingers over the worn surface as the cook, Mrs. Halsey, looked at the picture first, taking it in her hand and holding it at arm's length.

She shook her head. "They run in and out of here; you know how it is. Maybe I seen her, maybe I didn't. But I don't think so."

I took the picture back and handed it to Jennifer. "How about you?" I asked. "You think you ever saw her?"

She walked away from her boss and bent her head over the picture, looking at it intensely, perhaps because she had never seen a snapshot of a dead person. "Maybe," she said, coming back. "Maybe I saw her outside."

"Was she a novice or a student?" I asked, giving her the only choices.

She shook her head. "Not a novice. You can hardly see their faces anyway the way they walk. She'd've been a student."

"Thanks, Jennifer."

It didn't mean she was a student, just that she dressed like one. If you saw a girl in street clothes on campus, you assumed she was a student at the college. And there had been secular clothes in the duffle bag I had looked through.

From there I went to the laundry. One of the charges of a nun might be to run the washing machines on a particular day, then fold the laundry and distribute it. Habits were generally shared, a nun picking up as many as she needed for the coming week. There was no way of knowing when Anita had acquired her habit but if she hadn't actually taken it from the real Tina's room or from the room of another novice, I could think of no other source. The convent orders habits from a distributor and they are sent by mail or by a package service. You can't exactly walk into Bloomingdale's or Sears and buy a Franciscan habit.

All the washing machines were going when I walked in. A nun was pulling clothes out of a dryer and I waited for her to turn around.

"Kix!" she said, calling me by my old nickname. "Where's the little one?"

It was Sister Magdalena, a woman about sixty whom

I'd known since I went to live at St. Stephen's. "He's having a good time with Angela. How are you?"

"My knees hurt. I bet you've heard me say that before."

"Only about a hundred times. Maybe you shouldn't be doing work that makes you bend and lift."

"Oh, it's better that I do it. My knees are already gone. No sense making someone else suffer." She grinned at me and picked up a plastic laundry basket and set it on a table, ready for sorting.

"I want to ask you if you saw the girl in this picture." I held it so she couldn't see it. "She's dead in the picture. I want you to prepare yourself."

"Well, we've been hearing about this all morning, I guess. Let me see it."

I handed it to her. She wore large bifocals and she peered through them at the black-and-white face.

"She could be a student. I don't know many of them anymore. You should really talk to Sister Bernadette. She's in the laundry more than I am. Is it the laundry you're interested in?"

"I think she may have taken a novice's habit."

"So that's where it went."

"Where what went?"

"One of the novices said she was missing a habit after the others took theirs."

"How long ago was that?"

"Oh, maybe a week, maybe ten days."

"And they never found it?"

"Not that I heard. You ask Sister Bernadette. She'll tell you."

"Where can I find her?"

She looked at the big round clock on the wall. "I'd guess she's setting the tables for lunch right now."

"Thanks. You're a doll."

"That's what they all say," she said, her face all lit up. "That's what they all say."

I found Sister Bernadette exactly where I had been told to look. She was distributing silverware in the dining room for the noonday meal and she dropped a bunch of it noisily when she looked up and saw me.

"I saw Angela walking around with a little boy so I figured you might be around. I didn't think he'd come up here by himself yet."

"Not quite yet. How are you doing?"

She told me in some detail, making light of a problem that had hospitalized her a few months ago. The average age of this convent was getting older and older as the number of novices declined and the women who had been vigorous forty-five-year-olds when I came to live here were now in their sixties and somewhat less vigorous.

When we had finished our chat, I told her about my conversation with Sister Magdalena and showed her the picture.

"I probably saw her," she said, studying the picture. "But I couldn't swear to it. There are always groups of girls walking around the grounds."

"Then she was a student."

"If I saw her, I saw her with the students. But I don't know her name."

"Sister Magdalena told me a novice's habit was missing a week or two ago from the laundry."

"Yes, it was. I remember that. It never turned up. One

of our girls went to pick up her fresh laundry and she was one short."

"Did anyone ever ask you where to find a habit?"

"Who would ask? If you live here, you know where to look."

That was surely true. I was about to say good-bye when Angela dashed in, carrying Eddie.

"Chris, Chris, I've been looking all over for you. Joseph said to tell you that Tina came back last night and you can talk to her anytime you want."

"That's great. Where can I find her?"

"I think she's in her room."

She told me the number and I went upstairs. Eddie would eat with Angela and then she would see if he would nap. In the meantime, I was happy for the opportunity to talk to the real Tina Richmond.

I tapped on her door and she called, "Come in."

There was no similarity between her looks and those of the imposter. The real Tina was heavier and darker than the girl we had met. Her face was fuller, her eyes were brown, and she had none of the other girl's paleness and fragility. I told her who I was and she said Sister Joseph had filled her in on some of what had happened.

We sat down, she on the bed and I on the desk chair. I took the picture out and showed it to her.

She nodded. "I know who she is. We were in a class together."

"Did she tell you her name?"

"Randy something. I don't know if she ever told me her last name."

"Was her name called on the roll?"

"I don't think so. I think she just sat in on classes sometimes."

"Where did she live?"

"I'm not sure. She was kind of weird. I think she worked in town. Maybe in a bakery."

"So you never met her family."

"No."

"Did she tell you anything at all about herself?"

"Nothing that I can remember."

"Did she drive to the convent, Tina?"

"She must have. How else could she have gotten here? It's an awfully long walk from most of the town and it's all uphill."

"Did you notice her with anyone else? Did she mention any friends at the college?"

"No. We talked mostly about the class. And she asked me a lot of questions."

"What about?"

"About being a novice, what we did, how we lived, what our rules were. I thought she might be interested in becoming a nun."

"Anything else?"

"She asked about some of the nuns, what they were like."

"Do you remember which ones?"

"Sister Joseph, some of the others. And she wanted to know about the Villa, who lived there."

It sounded to me as though the imposter had picked up a lot of useful information from Tina. "Sister Joseph said you lost your purse. Can you tell me about it?"

"I was carrying a lot of things and I must have left it behind somewhere. I went back to all the places I could remember being and it wasn't there. I was really lost. It had all my identification and I knew I was going home for the Mother's Day weekend and I might need it."

"What did you do?"

"I got another college ID before I left."

"The girl in that picture was carrying your purse."

She looked at me. "You think she stole it from me?"

"She got it somehow. Do you remember the last time you saw her?"

"I really don't. But it was more than a week ago, I think."

"Is it possible that the last time you saw Randy was when you missed your purse?"

She thought about it. "It could have been. This is awful. Why would she want my purse? I didn't carry much money in it. Anyone who knows novices knows they don't have a fortune with them."

"It may have been the ID that she wanted. Tell me, Tina, did you know who I was before today?"

"I've heard your name mentioned. I think I saw you once when you came up with your little boy."

"Did you know where I lived?"

"No."

"Did Randy ask you about me?"

"Not that I remember."

I heard bells and I looked at my watch. "It's lunchtime and I don't want to keep you. If you think of anything else, I'll be here for a while this afternoon and Sister Joseph can always get a message to me. I hope you're happy at St. Stephen's."

She smiled. "I am. Very happy."

"Good. I'm glad to hear it."

* * *

I joined Joseph in her office for lunch. It had just arrived when I got there and she had the long conference table set up with our trays.

"Your motel room seemed very nice. I hope you slept well," I said when we sat down.

"I did, but I had that poor girl on my mind. There was a call for you from Jack a little while ago. I didn't know where you were so I talked to him. Detective Joe Fox called him this morning and said Jack's fingerprints and the girl's fingerprints were on the ax."

"I'm not surprised." I looked at the tray with appreciation. There was a cup of wonderful-smelling soup, a salad with chicken, a soft roll and butter, and some cookies. Joseph had a carafe of fresh coffee for our empty cups.

"I've just been talking to Tina Richmond. She knew the other girl and said her name was Randy. She really didn't know much else about her. She said they talked about the class. This Randy appeared to be auditing it. Her name was never called on the roll."

"So she must have followed Tina one day to see where she was going because she knew she wanted to play the part of a novice."

"She also asked questions about being a novice and about some of the nuns. Tina remembers that your name came up."

"That fits with what we know."

"Why did she pick me to come to?" I asked.

"Perhaps she knew we were friends."

"I wonder if she was living with someone nearby. She certainly wasn't living at the convent."

"It's hard to find out when we don't have a name. If she rented a room in town, who would notice she was gone until the next rent day?"

"Joseph, do you have any empty rooms in the dorm?"

She left the table and went to the file cabinet near her desk. She pulled a folder from a drawer and brought it back to our table. "You're thinking she might have been a squatter in an empty room?"

"It's possible. We should certainly look into it."

"Last semester we were filled to capacity but one student left at Christmas and didn't come back and one girl fell ill a month or so ago and went home. It may have been mono or something like that and her family thought she should rest at home."

"I'd like to see those rooms when we've finished our lunch."

"That's easy." She looked through the folder. "And there are two rooms under renovation, which means there are men in there weekdays between nine and five."

"I'll look at those, too."

Joseph made some notes. "If your suspicions are true, it would make her sound quite devious."

"Resourceful," I said.

"Where would she have gotten the key to such a room?"

"Where did she find my name and address? Where did she find a novice's habit?"

"You're right. She was resourceful. I hope we find out who she was. She must have a family somewhere."

I agreed. Whoever they were, wherever they lived, they would want to know what happened.

12

Armed with the master key, I walked over to the college dormitory when we finished our lunch. It was the end of the semester and girls were finishing exams and getting ready to leave for the summer. I went up to the second floor and down the long hall, hearing pieces of conversations from the rooms I passed. From one came the sound of wailing: "I'll never get it. I'll never get it. Why do I have to take this stuff? I'm not going to be a chemist if I live a hundred years."

I had felt much the same way myself about chemistry but I had managed to pass. The room I was looking for was the last one on the right, a corner room with, as it happened, a window on each outside wall, a very desirable place to live.

"She's not there," a girl said, and I turned.

"Who isn't?" I asked.

"Amanda Snyder. She got mono and she left."

"Anyone else been using her room?"

"Not that I know of."

She watched me as I turned the key. "Thank you," I said, letting myself in.

It was about the size and shape of the nuns' rooms

and with similar furniture. I opened the closet and found it empty. The bed had a cover on it but there were no sheets underneath. The desk had nothing on it but a lamp in one corner, and the drawers were empty except for dust and ink stains and eraser tidbits. I carefully removed each drawer and looked underneath, then into the drawer space itself. Nothing. A similar search of the dresser yielded only an old stamp, not enough to post a current letter. I got down on the floor and peered under the bed. Dust floated there and a piece of paper lay among the balls. I stretched my right arm as far as I could and just barely touched it. I flattened myself, got my shoulder under the bedframe, and snared the paper between my first two fingers and pulled it out.

I blew the dust off, making myself cough. The note was written in ballpoint and said, "Dr. Cabot, 3 P.M. Thursday." Probably the appointment that led to the student's departure from the college. But just in case, I put it in my bag, brushed myself off, and left the room.

The two rooms being renovated were on the third floor as was the other empty room. I went up the concrete stairs and found the two rooms side by side in the middle of the corridor. Two men were in the first room I reached, talking and working. I stepped inside.

"Hi. Can I talk to you a minute?"

"Sure." The older man came down off a ladder where he had been standing with a paint roller, working on the ceiling. "Something we can do for you?"

"Just a couple of questions. What time do you get here in the morning?"

"We don't come till nine. The Reverend Mother doesn't want us around while the girls are dressing and getting ready for class."

"And when do you leave?"

"Five, maybe four-thirty. Depends how we're doing."

"What have you been doing besides painting?"

"There was some water leakage. We had to find it, stop the leak, and repair the damage. This wall here was replastered like the one in the room on the other side."

"How long've you been working on that?"

" 'Bout a month. These rooms were empty because of the water."

"I want to ask you a funny question. Is there any chance someone could have been living in one of these rooms at night while you were working on them during the day?"

"In here?" He looked around at the four walls as the other man put his tool down and stood up. "I don't know how anyone could live here. There's no bed or nothin'. We got drop cloths all over. It smells of paint now and it smelled of plaster last week."

The younger man rubbed his hands on his work clothes. "You think someone's been camping out in here?" he asked.

"I thought it was a possibility."

"I don't think so."

I took the picture out of my bag. "Either of you ever see her? This was taken after she died."

"She died?" the older man said.

"Over the weekend."

They both looked at it, then gave it back, the older man distinctly paler. I thanked them and looked for the last empty room. It was just on the other side of the stairway. The key got me in and I closed the door behind me.

This room, too, had a covered bed with no bedding, a desk, and a chair. The desk was empty. I went over to the dresser and pulled open one drawer after another. In the top drawer I found some socks and underwear. In the second drawer there were a couple of nightshirts, two cotton blouses, and a pair of black sweatpants. The other drawers were empty. I repeated my previous search, drawers out, over, inspect cavity, with the same result: no secrets.

I went to the closet and found a raincoat, a pair of sneakers, and a skirt. There was no light in the closet so I got down on my haunches and felt around the floor. Near the back wall I felt something. Pulling it out I saw that it was a backpack-style purse. By this time I was feeling very excited. I slipped on the gloves I had in my pocket, opened the purse, and went through it. There was a worn wallet with no money. I assumed the money had been transferred to Tina's bag. There was a ball-point pen, some tissues, a mirror from a hardware store, a half ticket that could have come from a local movie, a couple of paper clips and safety pins, and two envelopes that looked like handwritten personal letters.

Before opening them, I went through the wallet carefully. Sure enough, there was a Social Security card for Randy Collins. I put everything back in the bag and took it with me. As I locked the door, a girl walked by.

"Excuse me," I said, stopping her. "Have you ever seen this girl? She died over the weekend."

She took the picture in her hand and looked at it seriously. "Was this taken after she was dead?"

"Yes."

"I think I've seen her around. I don't know who she is."

"Thank you." I tucked the picture in my bag and went down the stairs to the first floor and out to the campus. The spring air was delightful and I inhaled deeply as I hurried along the walks to the Mother House.

Eddie was sleeping soundly in Angela's room. Because he was lying on a bed, she was nervous about leaving him, so she sat in her room and read while he slept. When I tapped on her door, she tiptoed out and told me how good he had been. I always know if I need my spirits boosted, this is the place to come.

From there I went to Joseph's office. She was on the phone but got off quickly.

"Look what I found," I said, setting the backpack on her desk.

"Our imposter was living in one of those rooms?"

"She sure was, the one on the third floor. She has clothes hanging in the closet and in the top two drawers of the dresser. There's no question in my mind she intended to come back there."

"Amazing. I've been congratulating myself on our security and here someone has breached it in a very big way."

"Very big indeed. But it's because she was young and female that she was able to do it. She must have had a key for the room because it was locked when I got there. I guess she just kept quiet, didn't have a radio or TV, no phone, nothing to make noise. If she came and went while the downstairs doors were unlocked, who would notice her? She was the right age, she wore the same kinds of clothes as the students. I asked a girl in the hall if she recognized her and she said she'd seen her around."

"But she didn't say she lived in that room and her name was whatever."

"No. And the name on her Social Security card is Randy Collins."

"Chris, this is really a huge step forward. Do you have an address or is that too much to ask?"

I put my gloves back on and Joseph laughed. I took out the two envelopes in the backpack. "I haven't looked at these yet." I slid a letter out of the smaller one and read it aloud: "Sweetheart, Have a happy birthday. Spend this any way you want. Dad."

"Is there a return address?"

"No. And the postmark's very faint. But it's addressed to Miss Randy Collins on a street in Albany."

"What's the other letter, Chris?"

"The envelope's empty," I said, sounding my disappointment. "It's addressed to the same place and the postmark is Albany."

"I bet our mysterious Randy Collins is a student up there, maybe at the Teachers College. I think their semester ends a little before ours."

"So she took her birthday check from her father and got on a train down the Hudson. Maybe she told her parents she wanted to visit New York City before coming home for the summer."

"Let's see that envelope from her father," Joseph said. "I've got a magnifying glass in here somewhere. Maybe we can figure out where the letter comes from."

She rummaged around and pulled out a round glass with a black wooden handle. It looked very old. The glass was held in place with a heavy brass collar. Then she joined me on the other side of the desk so we could look through it together.

"I've never really gotten used to these two-letter abbreviations," she said. "I suppose it's a sign of age but I really liked the old way better. What do you think?"

"I think they should have inked their meter," I said. "It's N something. Could be New York, New Jersey, New Hampshire."

"I agree. The city is illegible. I suppose the police have ways of bringing out the print."

The phone on her desk rang and she leaned across to pick it up. It was a short conversation. "Detective Fox is here, Chris," she said when she was finished.

"Oh dear."

"Well, you've done his work for him. You've found out who she is and where she was living. I'd better get downstairs and make sure this is done in an orderly way."

"And I'd better pick up my son and get going. I'll leave the backpack and the master key with you. You can take it from there."

"I'll call you if we learn anything. Thanks for coming, Chris."

I managed to avoid Detective Fox on my way out. Eddie was awake and visiting the Villa with Angela. The Villa is where the retired nuns live and collectively they're like a group of grandmothers. I wasn't sure who was entertaining whom more. Eddie didn't want to leave and I didn't want him bursting into tears in front of all these women who thought so well of both of us. Finally, two of them said they would walk us to the car and Eddie held their hands as we went.

"They stole him from me," Angela mourned.

We both laughed. "We'll be back. I hear the detective on the case has arrived. He'll probably be asking everyone questions."

"I have no answers," Angela said. "He can save his time."

The sun was warm when we got to the parking lot. Eddie gave a lot of kisses and I did the same. Stuffed in his bag of tricks were cookies and brownies for later. We both waved as I backed out of my spot and started out of the convent grounds unseen, I hoped, by the good detective.

Eddie was running around in his pajamas, waiting to see whether Daddy or bedtime would arrive first, when the doorbell rang. Through the living-room window, I could see a car parked in front of the house. I opened the front door and Detective Fox was standing on my doorstep.

"OK, Mrs. Brooks," he said, raising his hands in a classic Wild West gesture of surrender, "you win. Can we talk about it?"

"Win what? Come on in. I don't know what you're talking about."

"You were at St. Stephen's today, right?"

"Yes. I drove up this morning with my son."

"And you told the nuns not to talk to me."

"What? No. I would never do that." I felt confused. "Let's sit down. Would you like some coffee?"

"I would love some coffee. It's been a hell of a day."

I showed him to the family room and told Eddie who he was. Although I found Detective Fox rather disarming, Eddie found him a little scary. He clung to me as I made coffee. Finally, he said he wanted to go to bed and I took him upstairs.

When I came down the coffee was ready. I hadn't eaten yet but I joined the detective with a cup. "The nuns wouldn't talk to you?" I said.

"Sister Joseph did. She showed me the room you'd found where our victim apparently was squatting. That was a good idea you had, looking in plain sight. Now at least we know who she is and we're going to notify her family. But no one else up there would say a word. They said they didn't know anything or that it was your case and you'd take care of it."

I stifled a giggle. "They really don't know anything," I said, trying to soothe his feelings. "I only talked to a couple of the nuns and they didn't have much to tell me. I suspect the victim, Randy Collins, stayed in that room at night and left in the morning when most of the other students were gone."

"You're telling me you didn't ask them not to co-operate."

"I would never do that," I said. "My husband is a police officer. It would be disloyal of me to do something like that. And I have no reason to."

"Let me ask you something I haven't asked you before. When did you call Sister Joseph yesterday to tell her that a girl you thought was a novice had been murdered?"

"I'm not sure. It was all so hectic. It was after we came back from mass."

"So what are we talking? Nine? Ten? Eleven?"

"I think we went to church at nine, so I would have called her about ten, maybe a little later."

"And she was there when you called."

"Yes."

"OK, so by ten she was back at the convent."

"What do you mean, 'back at the convent'?"

"She wasn't there earlier."

"Detective Fox, you said the nuns wouldn't talk to you. Now you tell me they said Joseph wasn't at the convent yesterday morning. I don't understand."

"Father Kramer didn't see her. He talked to me."

I felt the seeds of panic inside me. "What are you saying?"

"I'm saying she can't account for her time Sunday morning. I'm saying she could have been in Oakwood early Sunday, gotten back to the convent by the time you called, and come down here to identify the dead girl."

"Why would she have been in Oakwood early Sunday morning?" I asked, keeping my voice as even as I could manage.

"You're the smart one. Put it together. This girl knew something that could damage the sister's life and career. The girl calls the sister and says she's willing to talk about it, the sister drives down, maybe picks up the girl in front of your house early in the morning, and—"

"I don't want to hear any more of this," I said, feeling angry and betrayed. "Sister Joseph told you something, a fictional story concocted by a disturbed young woman, in order to keep me from being put on the spot. Now you're using that story, for which you have not the slightest proof of its truth, to make her seem like the worst sort of criminal. You should be ashamed of yourself."

"Calm down, Mrs. Brooks. Let's not forget that a girl

was murdered, that someone aimed a gun at her and pulled the trigger. She's dead. Let's keep that in mind. Your husband's prints are all over the ax that was found out by that tree."

"So were hers," I interjected.

"So were hers, I'll grant you that. But I can make a case that your husband killed her. He not only owns guns, he knows how to use them."

"That's absurd."

"To you it may be absurd. To me it's a line of inquiry. But I don't think your husband had anything to do with it. I do think there's a possibility that Sister Joseph, who has a strong motive to keep that girl quiet, could have."

I can hardly explain how I felt. I wanted to scream at him. I wanted to kick him out of my house and lock the door after him permanently. I think I actually wanted to hit him. I did none of those things. I controlled my mouth, my breathing, and my hands. I made sure I did not cry, which would have embarrassed me to no end. I was about to say something when he said, "I've made you very angry."

"Angrier than I can remember ever feeling. I think you should leave, Detective Fox. You have totally betrayed my trust and Sister Joseph's. I am through cooperating. I have nothing else to say to you so there's no reason for you to be here."

"I wanted to congratulate you on finding where that girl was staying."

"You don't have to congratulate me for anything."

"It shows you're smart. I'm not sure I would have thought of looking on campus for her."

"I have experience. I use it."

"We're not charging anyone at the moment. But if we do, I'll be back."

"Forget it. You're not welcome here." I stood and went to the living room, the detective following me.

"I have a feeling I've handled this badly," he said.

"Take your feelings and go, please. I hope you come to your senses. You will never find Randy Collins's killer if you continue looking for him at St. Stephen's. That's a guarantee." I opened the front door. "Good night, Detective Fox."

"Good night, Mrs. Brooks. I'm sorry to have upset you."

I closed the door with more pressure than I needed and I turned the bolt. Without looking out the window, I could hear the car in front of the house start up and drive away.

This was simply crazy. I knew I was overwrought but my distress was justified. Joseph was as good a human being as anyone I had ever met. I knew that good people sometimes did bad things but I knew, too, that she would not. The very fact that she had told Detective Fox about Randy Collins's ravings demonstrated her integrity. I knew it was dangerous to vouch for another person, but I would vouch for Joseph before anyone else I knew.

I am aware that the day may come when my son comes home and tells me lies about where he has been and what he has done. I am sure my heart will break if and when that happens. But Joseph would not lie to me.

I went upstairs and looked in on Eddie. He was fast asleep, the picture of innocence. I felt tears in my eyes, a combination of the anger I had felt a few minutes before and the peace that now came over me. I stroked Eddie's hair. It was still so soft and silky.

A car pulled into the driveway. I left the room, closing the door behind me. Jack was home and I would have to tell him what had happened.

13

"He said what?" Jack was carrying the jacket he had worn to work, along with a briefcase that he now frequently took with him.

"I was so angry I threw him out. I wasn't polite, I wasn't nice, I wasn't cooperative. I just wanted him out."

"You did the right thing. You don't have to cooperate. I think you should call Sister Joseph and tell her what Fox told you and then think about calling Arnold. He's good and he knows her."

"OK."

"You look all worn out."

"I feel that way. This has just been devastating."

"I'll be down in five minutes and we can eat. It'll give me a little more time to think."

Our dinner was nice and easy, leftovers from yesterday's wonderful banquet. Fortunately, all I had to do was reheat, and in the condition I was in, that was taxing enough. By the time we had finished eating and Jack had heard all about my day, we had decided I should call Joseph and tell her what Detective Fox had said and ask her if she wanted me to call Arnold. Arnold is Arnold Gold, not only a great defense attorney but a dear friend since I left St. Stephen's, a mentor to Jack, and an admiring acquaintance of Sister Joseph.

Jack took over the dishes and I started with Joseph. It took a few minutes for the evening switchboard operator to locate her, but finally she came to the phone.

"We had quite an afternoon with Detective Fox," she said, sounding her usual calm self. "I'm not sure he left knowing any more than when he arrived, except that I told him what you'd learned and gave him the backpack you found in Randy Collins's room."

"He ended up on my doorstep this evening," I said. "Did he talk to you today?"

"He asked me a few questions, but mostly he was interested in what you'd discovered. He sealed up the room that Randy stayed in. He's sending over a crime-scene unit tomorrow morning to go through it. I told him we couldn't have men walking around the dormitory at night."

"Joseph, I don't know how to say this. Detective Fox thinks you could have committed the murder."

There was hardly a beat before she said, "Well, he must really be at a loss. I didn't go to Oakwood till you called me and I gather she had been dead for several hours by then."

"He says you can't account for your time yesterday morning. Joseph, you don't have to give me any explanations. I believe you and I threw him out of my house. Jack thinks that one of us should call Arnold Gold. You may need the protection of a good lawyer."

This time there was a pause. "If Jack thinks so, I'll take his advice."

"Would you like me to call him for you?"

"Yes. Thank you."

"I'm sorry to have upset you. Detective Fox was peeved that none of the nuns would help him. I told him they didn't know anything, but even so, he thought I had put them up to it, not answering his questions. I told him he'd never solve this murder if he kept looking for a killer at St. Stephen's."

"You're right, but I don't like this new turn of events."

"I'll have Arnold call you as soon as possible."

In my book, Arnold is a great man. I'm sure there must be potential clients that he turns down, but I have seen him take on cases that were lost causes and win them. He is a firm believer in the Constitution and he doesn't get on well with the police if they try to circumvent the law.

Besides all that, he has been very good to me, so much so that I have come to consider him a surrogate father. He gives me work when he has it and included me in his office health plan until I married Jack, to make sure I was covered. When I left St. Stephen's, there were a number of things I had very little knowledge about and I was grateful that he looked out for me.

He met Joseph at our wedding, which was at St. Stephen's, and he was greatly impressed with her knowledge and wisdom, as she was with his. I knew what I was going to tell him would distress him, but there was no choice.

I called him at home and had a quick chat with Harriet, his wonderful wife. He came on the line with a breezy, "So, what's up? Baby OK? Jack doing well?"

"Everyone's OK, Arnold. It's good to hear your voice. I'm afraid I need your help. You're not going to believe what I'm about to tell you."

He must have sat down at that point and turned down the music. There is always music in the background when I talk to Arnold. His life is incomplete without music. I think that's wonderful.

I started at the beginning with the girl in a novice's habit appearing on my doorstep less than a week ago and finished with the visit from Detective Fox this evening.

"I don't want to hear any more," he said as I took a breath. "Give me Sister Joseph's phone number. Can I reach her now?"

"I'm sure you can. And if the switchboard is closed, calls go directly to her room. She'll answer."

"Are you going to continue working on this, Chris?"

"I don't think I have a choice now. I've got to prove that this defamatory story is wrong and I'd like to find out who killed that poor girl."

"They'll probably come together at some point. It sounds as though you may have to travel to talk to some of those people. How're you going to manage?"

"I really don't know. I just know that this is too important to leave to the professionals."

I heard a chuckle. "Good point. OK. Let's say good night and let me call before those nuns all go to sleep. Thanks for bringing me in on this. Even though I feel my blood pressure going up, I'm rarin' to go."

Nothing new as far as I could see. But I felt much better when I hung up.

Almost as soon as I was off the phone, it rang. Jack did me a favor and picked up. It was for him and as he spoke, I realized he was talking to Detective Fox. Happy that I had avoided even the required pleasantries at the start of a conversation, I leafed through the *Times* and then picked up scattered toys.

Jack got off the phone and joined me in the family room while I was on my hands and knees. "Joe Fox," he said as I scrambled up. "He offers you a heartfelt apology for the misunderstanding he caused when he was here."

"There wasn't any misunderstanding."

"What else could he say? He's in a box. He went back to his office after his ordeal with the nuns and then you—I had to laugh when he said the nuns wouldn't talk to him."

"They don't know anything, Jack."

"Anyway, the autopsy on Randy Collins was done today and the report was on his desk. The single bullet could have come from the missing gun that our neighbor, Mr. Kovak, owned and allegedly lost. A Smith and Wesson Chief model, Z barrel, same caliber, thirty-eight with a standard lead round-nosed bullet. Nothing exotic there. It could have been fired from any one of about half a million handguns. The clincher here would be to find the gun, do a few test firings, and match the known bullets with the recovered bullet. If the grooves are the same, the lab technician can testify as to the match. But we still don't know whose finger pulled the trigger, or why. If it was Kovak's gun, he'll have a major problem. Ballistics can tell you a lot about the weapons, but not much about the people who use them. What else?" He had taken notes on the back of an envelope, more my style than his. "She was killed about six yesterday morning, give or take an hour. She hadn't eaten anything since the night before.

"Then he said he'd spoken to Randy's parents. Needless to say, they were shocked out of their minds. Randy has been a student at an Albany college for two years, a pretty good student, they said. They told Joe she was adopted when she was about a week old. They have no idea who her natural mother was but they said Randy had expressed some interest in finding out for herself. They neither encouraged nor discouraged her. They believe she was a happy, well-adjusted young woman and they don't know what she was doing in Oakwood or anything else that happened in the last few days. I guess he didn't tell them about her taking a room at St. Stephen's. What he told them was enough for one night."

"How did they account for her not being at the college she was attending?"

"I think you put your finger on it the other day. She had finished her exams and told them she was visiting a classmate in New York or near New York. She didn't give them a phone number but she called every day and said she was fine and having a good time."

"And meanwhile she was at St. Stephen's finding an empty room, making friends with Tina Richmond, and stealing a novice's habit. I guess parents believe what they want to believe."

"She also told them she might look for a job in New York for the summer. That gave her a good excuse for not coming home."

"She must have decided to play the part of a novice because she guessed I'd be more receptive to that than to a kid who landed on my doorstep with a wild story about Joseph."

"Sounds reasonable."

"Jack, I don't know how I'm going to do this, but I've got to talk to this Mrs. DelBello from the adoption agency. And see where that leads me. I don't think Detective Fox is interested in that, except for giving Joseph a motive for murder."

"He said Sister Joseph couldn't account for her time Sunday morning."

"She doesn't have to account for her time," I said, raising my voice in uncharacteristic anger.

"Cool down, honey. I know she doesn't, and that's what Arnold will probably say. But from a cop's point of view, if he has someone with a motive, the unaccounted-for time gives her opportunity. He can't let it pass just because you and I are convinced his suspect couldn't and wouldn't have done it."

"Which leaves me with a double mission. I have to prove Joseph didn't give birth to Randy and then I have to figure out who killed Randy so that he'll leave Joseph alone."

"Try the telephone," Jack said, suggesting the easiest first step. "If it turns out you have to go out there, we'll worry about it later."

"I'm teaching tomorrow morning, so Eddie will be with Elsie. I'll come home when I'm done and start making calls. What a mess, Jack. What an unbelievable mess."

I have been teaching a course in poetry at a nearby college since I left St. Stephen's. It's a small income, which I used to live on but now put away for Eddie's future. My purpose when I began was equally to earn something and to use my mind. Even though there are several times a year when the load of correcting papers and making up finals threatens my stability, for the most part it's a godsend. I dip into a world that is different from the Oakwood world, one that is stimulating and enjoyable. I have never had a class that I didn't find a pleasure to teach, and I enjoy interacting with the faculty. And although I would not put this first on the list of reasons why I continue to teach, I do get pleasure out of eating in the college cafeteria where all the food is prepared by students in the food service department. I've even taken home an occasional fruit pie, the crust still warm.

When I finished my class on Tuesday morning, I had a good lunch and then went straight home, not stopping to do the usual shopping I try to accomplish before I pick up Eddie. That could all wait till later. I sat down with my notebook open in front of me and called information for the number of God's Love Adoptions.

That took only a few seconds. I breathed a sigh of relief, having worried that with adoptions down, they might have gone out of business. But they were there and someone answered and referred me to Debbie Wright, who picked up almost immediately.

It was a complicated story but I felt if I expected her to give me any help, I'd better tell a good part of it, so I did.

"You're telling me that the child has been murdered?" Ms. Wright said.

"She was shot on Sunday morning. I can refer you to our local police department. And she's not a child. She's twenty now."

"And you want me to help you find her birth mother."

"I'd like you to do as much as you can. Someone's life and reputation are at stake here."

"Those records are sealed, Ms. Bennett. You'd need a court order—You couldn't get a court order. You have no status in this case. I don't see how I can help you."

"Perhaps you can tell me how to reach Mrs. DelBello."

"Oh, Sophie. She retired a few years ago and she's not well."

"If I could just talk to her."

I heard a faint sigh. "She's really not at all well."

"Ms. Wright, if the police arrest an innocent woman for the murder of Randy Collins—"

"They suspect a woman?"

"A woman I know, a woman who is beyond reproach."

"What does this have to do with Randy's birth mother?"

"There's a link there and I've got to find out what it is. There are so many unanswered questions that it's hard for me to give you more information."

"Well."

I waited.

"Here's Sophie's phone number. If she wants to talk to you, it's up to her." She dictated a number without saying where it was.

I told her how much I appreciated her help and then I sat back looking at the number I had written. Sophie DelBello, retired, not well. OK, Kix, I said to myself. Let's do it.

The phone at the other end rang several times before it was picked up. It was a woman's voice and it wavered slightly.

"Mrs. DelBello?" I asked.

"Yes. Who's this?"

"My name is Chris Bennett. I'm calling to ask you about an adoption that took place about twenty years ago."

"Is this Randy?"

"No, it's Chris," I said, realizing she was recalling a

conversation with Randy Collins. "I met Randy last week. I'm sorry to tell you Randy died."

"Oh no. She was just a child."

"Yes, she was quite young. Mrs. DelBello, I need information on Randy's natural mother."

"I told her everything I knew. I don't know anything else. The records are at the agency and I wouldn't be able to tell you what was in them if I had them."

"I have some questions that I don't think she asked you."

"Please, this is very hard for me. I'm not in good health. Can you come over so we can talk face-to-face? My hearing isn't so good anymore and even holding the phone is hard."

I had to say it. I wasn't sure how I would manage, but there wasn't any choice. "I can come, but I can't get there till Thursday. I'm calling from New York."

"That's far away."

"If you can give me your address—"

She told me slowly where she lived in Ohio and how to get there from the airport. It was hard for her to get around, she said, so if it took a minute for her to get to her door, I should be patient. I promised I would.

When I got off the phone, I called Jack.

14

I am not a world traveler. I have neighbors who get on and off planes almost as frequently as I get in and out of my car. Business takes them across the country and sometimes across an ocean. I have flown very few times in my life and never since Eddie was born. I had never left him overnight. I didn't want to go, but I wanted to clear Joseph's name more.

Fortunately, Jack's current job requires no overtime and he agreed to drop Eddie off at Elsie's before work on Thursday and pick him up on the way home. I assumed I would be gone for one day, but just in case—Jack is the "just in case" man—I packed a small suitcase and made a hotel reservation that could be cancelled if I called by four in the afternoon. To be perfectly honest, he made the reservation because he had the credit card. That was another worry. What if I needed to pay for something and I ran out of money?

Sometimes I really get angry at myself. You're not a nun anymore, I said sternly as I went to collect Eddie after making a lot of phone calls. Why don't you take your place in the twentieth century before it becomes the twenty-first?

Jack saved the day, as he often does. When he came

home, he said he had a little present for me. It was indeed one of the smallest presents I had ever received. Apparently when he renewed his credit card, he asked for one for me and he put it away for a rainy day. Figuratively at least, it was pouring today.

"Have I told you you're wonderful?" I asked, looking at the plastic card with the little hologram in the corner.

"Don't worry about it. At work they fall all over themselves telling me how great I am. And I don't even give them plastic."

"I promise I won't be a spendthrift."

"Chris, you don't know how to be a spendthrift. Just keep it with you and use it when you have to."

I have to admit that having that little card gave me a sense of security that I had not had on a number of occasions. At least now I knew that I didn't have to worry about whether I could pay for the hotel if it turned out that I needed it. Or for a dinner that might cost more than I would ordinarily spend. I put the little card in my wallet and started to think about tomorrow.

I had not believed I could arrange my getaway quickly enough to leave on Wednesday, so I had a day free to use in Oakwood. The other side of this whole mess, if there was another side to it, was who had killed Randy Collins. On Wednesday morning I took Eddie and walked down the block to the Greiners' house.

Pine Brook Road is a pretty, curving street with houses on both sides. Some of the houses, like the one we live in, are fairly old and look like an earlier generation of building. But farther down the block where Mel and her family live, the land was developed later. I remember Aunt Meg saying how sad it was that those lovely old trees would be cut down for the new houses. That was a long time ago and those upstart houses are now twenty years old and many of them have had several owners. Some of the fine old trees were preserved and many new ones were planted and have achieved a great height and girth.

Mel's house is on the other side of the street from ours and its far property line is shared with the Greiners. Beyond the Greiners are the Kovaks. When Eddie and I reached Mel's driveway, Eddie turned into it.

"We're not going here today," I said.

"Wanna see Mel."

"Mel's not home. She's teaching."

"Wanna see Mel." He sounded angry.

"She's not there, Eddie."

But he kept going. OK, I thought. Time for a lesson. We got to the front door and I pushed the bell. We could hear it ring inside the house.

"See? She's not home."

He reached for the bell but missed it by a long way. I pushed it again and we waited. Finally I said I was going. I could see tears form. He waited a few seconds, then followed me.

"Mel isn't home," I said. "Maybe we'll see her this afternoon." I took a tissue from my pocket and patted the tears while he pulled his face away. Oh boy, I thought. And I'm going away tomorrow.

"Let's see if the Greiners are home," I said as we got to their house.

We turned up their driveway and walked to the front door. I pushed the bell and we waited.

The door opened and Carol Greiner, wearing jeans

and a man-tailored shirt tied at her waist, looked at us. "Chris," she said.

"Hi, Carol. Do you have a minute?"

She looked as though she wasn't sure. Then she said, "I can spare a minute. Come in."

She was a wiry, intense woman with a little gray in her hair, which she kept on the long side, usually tied back in a scruffy ponytail that did not show off her face to good advantage. The impression I usually had of her was that certain things took too much time so she didn't bother doing them, like making her hair look more flattering. She was on the right side of every cause in town. When I first moved to Oakwood and the question of allowing the residence for retarded adults came up, she was a loud and proud proponent. When the question of recycling grass and leaves was discussed, she said it would be money well spent. It had not been a surprise to me that she had fought for preserving a maple tree over someone else's driveway.

We went into her family room and she gave Eddie a cookie that she assured me had no sugar (he took one bite and put it down) and asked if I wanted a cup of caffeine-free tea. I knew she was just being polite so I turned down her offer.

"So what brings you here this morning?" she said, moving sections of newspaper out of the way.

"The girl who had the accident," I said, not wanting to be specific in front of my two-year-old, "was my guest for a couple of days and I feel duty bound to try to find out what happened."

"Isn't it obvious?"

"I don't think so."

"Stanley Kovak was cutting down the tree, she saw him, he—you know."

"It's possible but I don't think it happened that way. That was our ax that was found near the tree."

"Really? I hadn't heard that."

"I don't think it's definite but our ax is missing and the one they found has my husband's prints on it as well as the girl's."

"I see. You think she cut it down?"

"I think she may have."

"But why?"

"Mel and I told her about the problem the day before and she seemed distressed. I think she felt people should channel their energy into more worthwhile causes."

"That was a worthwhile cause," Carol said in a low voice.

"I'm just repeating what she said. She may have thought she would bring a resolution to the disagreement." I was trying to pick my words carefully. "Did the Kovaks ever tell you that their gun was missing?"

"That gun isn't missing. It's been hidden. It's their gun that did it."

"Did they ever talk about it?" I persisted.

"We don't talk about guns in this family."

"Did he ever mention owning it?" I asked.

"He did. He said he had it for protection. It made him feel safe."

"I didn't know he had a gun till Jack found out from the police."

"Well, you don't live next door to them. If you did, you would know."

"Besides this turmoil, are they good neighbors?"

She took a minute to consider, as though deciding

whether to say something nice about people that she obviously couldn't stand. "We haven't had any trouble. They take good care of their property. They don't make a lot of noise. They're pretty good neighbors." It had a grudging sound to it but I thought she was being honest. "I have to be somewhere," she said.

I stood and took Eddie's hand. "Thanks for your help. I don't suppose anyone in your family heard anything Sunday morning?"

"Nothing. We were all sleeping. Our bedroom is on the other side of the house and the boys sleep through everything, including alarms." She gave me a faint smile, the first time she had loosened up since we'd come in.

"Thanks, Carol."

Outside I asked Eddie, "Didn't you like the cookie?"

"No. Bad cookie."

I wondered if Carol's sons had accustomed themselves to sugarless cookies or if they got their sugar fix away from home.

We kept walking and turned up the Kovaks' drive, avoiding the raised area where the roots of the maple tree had done their deed. The Kovaks were somewhat older than their neighbors, having moved in when the house was first built, with young children who were now grown. They had a four-bedroom house just for the two of them, although I noticed that at least one daughter came to visit on weekends. Today the garage door was closed and I hoped they were home. I rang the doorbell and Mrs. Kovak opened it immediately.

"Hi, I'm Chris Brooks, your neighbor down the street."

"Yes, of course. Come in, please. I see you and your little boy all the time. He gets plenty of fresh air, don't you, dear?" She bent over to smile at him in a very grandmotherly way.

"Is your husband home?" I asked.

"Oh, yes. He's in the sunroom. You want to talk to him?"

"I'd like to talk to both of you."

We went into the sunroom at the back of the house. I am always intrigued at how people manage to personalize their homes, adding interesting rooms, decks, and patios, landscaping in unusual ways. The sunroom at the back of the Kovaks' house was not large but I could see why it was probably a favorite room. It was filled with beautiful green plants, some of them in bloom, and a small tree stood in a corner. The furniture was comfortable and whatever the season, there was a lovely view out the windows.

"Stanley, this is Chris Brooks, our neighbor. She lives in Margaret's old house." She turned to me. "Such a lovely woman, your aunt."

He looked up from a book he was reading, set it aside, and stood to greet us. Mrs. Kovak left for a moment, returning with a cookie for Eddie that I was sure was sweet. He took it, said thank you, and dug in.

"So," Mr. Kovak said, "to what do we owe the pleasure?"

"I want to talk to you about what happened on Sunday. The girl who had the accident was a guest of mine and I want to do everything I can to find out who was responsible."

"Well, we weren't."

"Do you have any idea who was?"

"Nope."

"Did either of you hear anything?"

"Nothing." His wife was silent.

"About your gun—"

"I don't have it. It was stolen, I reported it stolen, and I haven't seen it since."

"When did you buy it?"

"Oh boy. That's a good question. You remember when that was, Ellie?"

"Must be ten years ago."

"More. I don't remember. They have a record at the police station, unless they lost that, too. I did it on the up and up, got a license, bought the gun, just the way the law says you should."

"Where did you keep it?"

"Kept it in my bedroom. We've got a big closet and I had it wrapped in soft cloth, the way you're supposed to, up on a shelf where the grandkids couldn't reach it."

"Was it loaded?"

"I always kept one bullet in it."

"And you had other bullets besides?"

"Had a box of 'em. Kept it on the same shelf."

"The Greiners knew you had a gun, didn't they?"

"I didn't make no secret of it."

"When did you find it was missing?"

"When was that, Ellie?"

"It must be a month ago."

"More. Five or six weeks. I reached up to get something and I felt the cloth that I kept it in and didn't feel anything inside. I felt around and then I got a stepstool and climbed up to have a look. Took everything down from the shelf but it wasn't there."

"Was the box of bullets there?"

"It was there. I couldn't tell you if any of them were missing. I didn't count them."

"And you reported the loss to the police."

"I went over there myself the next morning. Gave them all the information, answered all their questions."

"And there's no record that you reported it," I said.

"Can't help it if they're incompetent." He seemed to shrug off the whole incident.

"Do you ever leave your door unlocked?" I asked.

A look passed between them and I sensed this was an issue they had talked about before. "I do," Mrs. Kovak said. She looked grim. "When we moved in, this was the safest place in the world. Everybody trusted everybody else. There wasn't any need to lock your doors."

"You can't trust everybody, Ellie. You know that."

"At first, I was very careful. I'd lock the door every time I went out because Stanley wanted it that way. We had bolts put on all the doors and I'd lock them, too. But after a while, it just didn't seem all that necessary. I remember once, I went somewhere and forgot to turn a tea kettle off so I called my neighbor—they're gone now—and asked her to go inside and turn off the stove. I'd left the back door open so it wasn't any trouble for her."

Stanley Kovak watched his wife as she told her story. His face was the picture of disapproval. I could sense her sadness that times had changed for the worse, that those friendly, trusting times were gone and you couldn't live with the same sense of security as in the good old days.

"Good cookie," Eddie said, beaming.

"Let me get you another one, dear. Why don't you come to the kitchen with me and you can pick one out." She seemed relieved to get out of the sunroom.

"So anyone could have walked in and found your gun," I said.

"Anyone who saw us leave the house. I work only part-time now, which is why I'm home this morning, but Ellie runs around, visits friends, goes shopping. If she doesn't lock the door, I tell you, it's asking for trouble."

Since I have a husband who feels essentially the same way, although he expresses himself rather less aggressively than Stanley Kovak, I felt some empathy for his point of view. "My husband is a police officer," I said. "He agrees with everything you say."

"Sounds like he has some sense. Can you tell me what all these questions are for?"

"I want to find out who killed that poor girl on Sunday morning."

"Well, you're lookin' in the wrong place. I hated that tree, hated what it did to my driveway, what it did to my cars every time you went over that cracked cement. I would've given a prize to anyone who'd cut it down. Why that girl did it, I can't tell you. I never saw her before I saw her dead."

"Had you been near an agreement with the Greiners on the tree?" I asked.

"There was some talk about getting in a professional mediator but nothing was settled. That's where I'd look for a killer, if I was you."

"At the Greiners'?"

"Who else?"

"Stanley," his wife said, coming back, holding Eddie's hand, "you shouldn't say that. They're decent people."

"Decent people sometimes go berserk. I think they saw what was going on and came out and shot her out of pure anger."

"Where did they get the gun?" I asked.

"Don't look at me. I didn't shoot anybody. They've got two big boys over there could've come in here and stolen the gun."

I didn't want to think about that. "I don't think they're people who have anything to do with guns," I said.

"That's the parents. You never know about the children."

I decided I had given him long enough on his soapbox. I stood and asked Eddie how he liked the cookie. He assured me it was very good and I wiped the crumbs off his face so we wouldn't leave a trail as we left. I thanked them both for their help, shook their hands to show them we were friends, and walked back to our house.

15

I sat beside a window on the plane the next morning with a breakfast tray in front of me, hoping all had gone well with Jack and Eddie. There was an empty seat to my left and a man with a laptop on the aisle. While he ate his breakfast, the laptop sat on the seat between us.

I had talked to Jack last evening about my interviews with Carol Greiner and the Kovaks. Jack was skeptical about the police losing a report of a missing gun but he said anything could happen and sometimes did, as he knew from thirteen years on the job. Still, it didn't seem likely.

We had no way of knowing whether it was the Kovak gun that had killed Randy Collins, only that the bullet in her came from the same caliber as the gun he had registered. And if the gun never turned up, we could never do the test firings and would never know for sure. There were plenty of handguns of that type around. And with the ax that was found at the crime scene almost certainly ours, it didn't make sense that Stanley Kovak had been the one to cut down the tree. The whole thing made me dizzy.

Ahead of me was a visit to a state I had never been in, which could describe most of the states in our country. I didn't have a lot of questions for Mrs. DelBello, but I thought that if we talked awhile, her memory might be jogged. If she could remember that Randy's natural mother was a petite blond or a sixteen-year-old red-head, that might be enough to get Joseph off the hook.

Jack had reserved a compact car for me at the airport and I followed Mrs. DelBello's directions to her home. I had called her last night and confirmed that I would see her today. She lived in a small house on a quiet street with similar small houses. Cars tended to be parked in garages or on driveways so there was plenty of room for mine right in front of her address.

I left my little suitcase in the trunk of the rental car, made sure I had the keys in my hand, and locked the doors. I rang the bell next to a door painted a beautiful shade of blue and waited.

The door eventually opened and a gray-haired woman with a sallow complexion, holding a cane, said, "You must be the lady from New York."

"I'm Chris Bennett. I'm happy to meet you, Mrs. DelBello."

We went inside, I following as she walked slowly. She didn't seem to need the cane to walk but probably took it for a sense of security. She sat in a firm chair and laid the cane on the floor beside her.

"Oh, I didn't take your coat."

"It's OK. I'll just leave it here. Please don't get up." I folded it over the back of the sofa and sat on a chair.

The room was clean and orderly and comfortably furnished, a carpet covering the floor and attractive draperies at the windows. There was a fireplace on one wall, the mantle covered with pictures from one end to the other.

"This is very comfortable," I said.

"I've lived here a long time. We raised three children here. My husband died several years ago and it looks like I don't have much longer myself, but I'll stay here as long as I can."

"How long did you work for God's Love Adoptions?"

"I went there as a girl doing secretarial work. While I was there, I took courses and got my degree in social work. From the beginning until I retired was forty-four years."

"You must have enjoyed the work," I said.

"Well, you're doing a service. On the one hand, there's a girl who's got a baby she can't bring up and on the other there's a couple that's desperate to have one. So you could say it's a double blessing."

"When did Randy Collins first come to you?"

"Oh, it's quite some time ago, a couple of years anyway. She wanted to find her birth mother. They all do nowadays. Back in the fifties, there was a lot less of that."

"What did you tell her, Mrs. DelBello?"

She looked down, as though getting her thoughts together. "Those records were sealed, you know."

"I understand. I'm not passing judgment."

"She came to our office and they said they couldn't help her. It's what we say when they come to us. I was still working there but I was close to retirement. I saw her when she came in. She seemed like a sweet girl. She cried when they turned her down. She was about to go and I got up from my desk and went to her. I said, 'Let's sit down and talk,' and we went back to my little cubicle. She was very grateful. I told her we couldn't give her information that we had promised to keep secret. She begged and pleaded and I left her for a minute and went to check the files. It had been one of my cases and I remembered it. I went back and told her I would do what I could and asked where I could call her. She gave me a number and said she was in Cincinnati for only a day or two. I walked her to the door and she left."

"Where was she staying?" I asked.

"I don't really know. When I called her, a man answered and called her to the phone. Maybe she was with a friend."

"Go on. I'm sorry I interrupted you."

She moved in her chair, making herself more comfortable. "I went to the files again later that afternoon. It was all there. I thought, well, I'll just give her the name of the hospital and she can take it from there. So that's what I did. She was born in Good Samaritan Hospital. It's outside the city. I called her that night and told her. She thanked me and said she would let me know how it turned out.

"But I didn't hear from her for a long time, months and months. Out of the blue she called me one day at home. I had retired by then and it took me a minute to remember who she was. She said she'd come to Cincinnati for the summer and got herself a job at the hospital. I said, 'Well, that's very enterprising of you,' and she said, 'I found the file of when I was born.' "

"How could she do that if she didn't know the name of her birth mother?"

"She found the file on herself. When she was adopted, she became Randy Collins. There was some cross-referencing that led her to her birth mother. There was a name and address and Randy went there and found a neighbor who put her in touch with the family. That's what she told me."

"Did she say she had found her mother?"

"Not yet. Her mother wasn't living in Ohio anymore."

"Did you ever hear from Randy again?"

"She sent me a Christmas card and said she was pretty sure she had found her mother and she was going to talk to her as soon as she could arrange it."

"And that was it?"

"That was it. I don't know what else I can tell you."

"I'd like to know what you remember about that adoption. You met the woman who gave birth, didn't you?"

"Oh, yes. She came to us when she was pregnant and said she was going to have a baby. She couldn't raise it herself, and she couldn't marry the father. She wanted to have it and give it up for adoption."

"She gave you her name and address and all that sort of thing?"

"Yes, she did. And proof of her age. She was old enough to do what she wanted."

"Where did she live while she was pregnant?"

"Oh, now I'm not sure I remember that. She may have lived at home."

"Did you ever call her there?"

"Yes. We kept in touch."

"Do you remember her name?"

"Bailey, I think it was. I remember that I called her Katherine."

I knew my shudder was visible.

"Are you all right, dear?"

"Yes, it's OK. I'm sorry. You were saying that you called her Katherine."

"That was her name."

"Do you remember what she looked like?"

"She was probably in her twenties. Medium hair. It wasn't blond, it wasn't red, it was just hair."

I smiled at that, sensing a description of myself. "Do you remember whether it was long or short?" This was a rather crucial question. The nuns at St. Stephen's have always worn habits and they keep their hair cut very short. Even if Joseph had been out of her habit for a few months when she first went to see Mrs. DelBello, her hair could not possibly be long.

"It was short, I remember that. She kept it neat. She was a neat-looking person. If you think she looked like a floozy, I can tell you she didn't."

"Do you know how tall she was?"

"She wasn't short. I'd say she was taller than me, but I'm not very tall myself."

Nothing she said was making me happy. "Do you remember if she wore glasses?"

"Oh, I think she did. Not all the time, you know, but she wore them."

Joseph wears them all the time now, but twenty years have passed. "Do you remember how she dressed?"

"It's twenty years, dear. I can tell you she didn't wear those miniskirts the girls were all wearing at that time. I remember when I met the prospective mother, she had on a skirt that left little to the imagination. But she was a nice woman and you can't make judgments on fashion. If you did, you'd rule out half the people in the world."

"How did it work, handing over the baby and all that?"

"The arrangements were all made before Katherine went to the hospital. She had the right to change her mind, but she seemed dead set against that. I notified the Collinses when she went in and they were in my office the next day."

"Did they ever get to see the birth mother?"

"We never allowed that. I brought the baby to them and they cried over her. She was such a pretty little thing." She sighed. "I can't believe she's dead, poor thing."

"Her parents are in shock," I said. "This has been a terrible blow."

"I can't think of anything worse."

"So they never met, the adoptive parents and the birth mother."

"Never. And the Collinses didn't know the name of the birth mother. Or the other way around. I assured Katherine that they were good Catholics—I checked up on that myself—and good people. And I told them that Randy's mother was a nice young woman who had made a mistake and wanted her daughter to grow up in a home with a father and mother and be well treated."

"Did Katherine ever tell you that she came from somewhere else? That she was leaving Ohio?"

"It never came up. What she did after she gave up her baby was her business."

"Did anyone visit her while she was in the hospital?" I asked.

"No one was ever there when I came to see her. I went a couple of times. I had to make sure her plans were firm."

"Did she share a room with anyone?" I asked, coming to the end of all my attempts to prove that the Katherine she was talking about was not Sister Joseph.

"It was a single room. She wanted it that way because of her situation. Imagine the pain of sharing a room with a woman whose husband comes to visit, a woman who knows she's taking her baby home with her."

"It must be terrible," I agreed. "Were you there when she signed the final papers?"

"I brought them over myself. She asked for a few minutes alone, I remember that—so she could read them over in private. She seemed very nervous. I left the room and went down the hall to the waiting room and gave her some time. When I came back, she was ready to sign. I asked her if she wanted to see the baby one last time, but she didn't. Some of them do, some of them don't. If you hold that baby enough, you won't want to give it up."

"I think you've answered all my questions," I said, not very happy with what I had learned.

"Can you tell me why you came all this way to ask them?"

"I think I know Katherine Bailey. She says she never had a baby out of wedlock."

"Well, it's twenty years, dear. I'm sure she's married now and she doesn't want her family to know. I understand how she feels. Let it be. What difference does it make?"

The difference between being indicted for murder and not, I thought. "You're probably right." I thanked her, told her to stay put, and went out to the car.

16

I drove a few blocks and pulled over to the curb. It was still late morning. I could get back to the airport and take an earlier flight and see my husband and child this evening, but nothing that Mrs. DelBello had told me had relieved my anxiety. While the description of the baby's mother was not a match for Joseph—no verbal description could have been—it was close enough to make me concerned. It certainly didn't rule out Joseph.

I had my notes and my file with me. I was reluctant to question Joseph's sisters because they would surely become very distressed at the direction of my queries, but if I had to, I would. There was the insurance office she had worked in and I could probably get there and back to the airport before my plane left. And then there was Joseph's cousin's son.

Jack and I had looked at a map together last night and I had a good idea of how to get to each of those places. I was hungry at this point and wanted to get some lunch before doing anything else, so I drove until I found a coffee shop and went inside with my file.

The waitress was very helpful and while I ate a fruit salad, I decided to try the insurance office. She directed me to the right highway and a few minutes after my lunch, I was on my way.

The insurance offices of Fine and Houlihan were on the second floor of an office building. I had not thought about it until that minute but it sounded like rather an ecumenical partnership. I took the elevator up and found the door with their names painted on frosted glass. Inside, a receptionist doing work at a computer asked who I wanted to see. I told her either Mr. Fine or Mr. Houlihan and she lifted the telephone.

"Mr. Fine will see you." She got up and directed me through a door into a large work area and then to another door.

Abraham Fine had a smile and a good handshake. He was about sixty, losing his graying black hair, and dressed in his shirtsleeves, wide suspenders on his shoulders. He was surrounded by files. The room was small but nicely carpeted and freshly painted. There were certificates framed on the wall and one window that brought light into the room.

"You are Christine Bennett?" he said.

"Yes. I flew in from LaGuardia this morning."

"That's a long way to go to buy insurance." He smiled broadly.

"You're right, and I hope you make it worth the trip." I sat in a chair opposite his desk and laid my file on the chair next to it.

"It looks as though you've done a lot of research. What brings you here?"

"I need some information, Mr. Fine. It's about a young woman who worked here for a while twenty years or so ago."

"That's a long time."

"I know, but it's very important. Her name was Katherine Bailey."

"Katherine Bailey, Katherine Bailey. You're right, it was about twenty years ago, but I remember her. Can you tell me why you flew in from LaGuardia to ask me about her?"

"I can tell you that I know her, that I admire her, and that she may be falsely accused of a terrible crime. What you remember about her may save her from that."

"Very interesting. Can I get you a cup of coffee?"

"No, thanks. I don't want to take up a lot of your time and I'm hoping to get back to my family this evening. I just want to know what you remember."

"Katherine was a lovely woman. She walked in here one day looking for a job because someone she knew had recommended us. I think we'd lost someone and had started looking around for a replacement. I liked her the minute I met her."

"She's a wonderful person," I said.

"She was very up front with us, said she needed a job for six months or a year and she'd be leaving after that. My partner, Jerry Houlihan, said it would be too much trouble to train someone for so little time, but I persuaded him. I just had good feelings about her. I didn't think she'd take a long time to learn what she had to do and I always thought, if she liked the work, maybe she'd stay."

"Yes," I agreed. "She certainly is a person that inspires confidence." I didn't bother mentioning that she had a job far away that was more than a job; it was a way of life.

"So I called her the next day and hired her."

"Do you remember how long she actually stayed here?"

"I'll find out. Give me a minute." He left the room and came back with a file folder. "We weren't very technologically sophisticated twenty years ago. All we had were paper records and this is her file." He sat at his desk and opened it, leafing through the pages inside. "Looks like she was here just a little less than a year."

"Was her health good? Did she call in sick very much?"

"I don't think she ever called in sick. What I do remember is that toward the end someone in her family died, I don't remember who. I don't think it was a surprise but it gave her a pretty hard time. She took off a couple of days when that happened. We didn't dock her pay. It was a family emergency and she was entitled to the time."

"Can you describe her to me?"

"A good-looking woman, but dressed very plain. Didn't wear a lot of makeup, maybe a little lipstick. Some of the girls here look as though they're going on stage. Not Katherine. She wore glasses most of the time, no jewelry. I don't think she was married. Said she was living with her family. I have the address here if you want it."

"Please."

He wrote it down and handed me the slip of paper. It was the address Joseph had given me for where her family had lived that year.

"Anything else?" I asked.

"She wore her hair kind of short and I remember that at that time all the girls were wearing it long. And her skirts were long when all the girls were wearing theirs short. I figured it evened itself out."

I smiled. "Did she change in any way that year?"

"Change? Like what?"

"Her looks, her behavior . . ." I let it hang.

"Can't say that she did. She looked about the same when she left as she did when she walked in that front door."

"What did you know about her, Mr. Fine? Besides her work in the office."

"Not much. I took her to lunch—Jerry and I both did—when she was getting ready to leave. That's about all the contact we had with her outside the office. But she was bright, I'll say that. And she was a pleasure to have around, did anything you asked her, learned quickly, filled in for people who were out sick.

"I did know one thing about her, come to think of it. She had been a nun somewhere. Did you know that?"

"I did know that."

"That's why—it comes back to me now—that's why her hair was so short. It grew in while she worked here, but it was always pretty short."

"So except for the hair, you think she looked the same when she left as when she came."

"Yeah, right. Is that important?"

"I don't know. It may be. Did you ever hear from her after she left?"

"Oh, sure. She sent us Christmas cards from some-place in New York. She went back to being a nun, you know."

I flipped a couple of pages in my notebook till I found the date of Randy Collins's birth. "Was Katherine working here in the month of May?"

"Oh, yes. She came in the fall and stayed through most of the summer."

"And the only time she took off was for that death in the family."

"That's right."

"I think that's it, Mr. Fine."

"That's it? You're done?"

"I think so."

"Hang on. You come in here and tell me Katherine Bailey's been accused of a terrible crime and that's it? You're not going to say anything else about it?"

"I'd rather not. She hasn't been accused and I'm hoping she won't be, because she hasn't done anything. If the worst happens, I promise I'll let you know."

"How did you happen to come to me?"

"She gave me your name. She said she enjoyed working here."

He smiled and he looked like a happy man. "I'm glad to hear that. I'm glad we felt the same way about each other."

We shook hands and he walked me to the door. Downstairs I found a pay phone and I called Jack.

"Hey, good to hear from you. How's it going?"

"Hard to tell. How's Eddie?"

"I just talked to Elsie. They're doing fine so stop worrying. Are you coming back tonight or don't you know yet?"

"I don't know yet. I've seen Mrs. DelBello and one of the partners in the insurance company Joseph worked for. I'm about to call one of her sisters. If she's not there, I'll probably go right to the airport."

"Well, don't rush home because of us. We guys know how to have fun without a woman around."

"I'm glad to hear it."

"I gotta tell you something. Joe Fox wants to check Sister Joseph's DNA against Randy Collins's."

"No!" I said it so fast it was out of my mouth before I knew I was going to say it.

"Why not? It's absolute. If Randy isn't related to Sister Joseph, that'll clear her."

"I don't want Joseph subjected to that. She said she wasn't Randy's mother. That's enough for me and that should be enough for the police."

"You sound like Arnold. That's just what he said."

I felt a sense of relief. "Good. He's right. I don't want her to be part of that."

"Chris, it's like fingerprints. If you weren't there, your prints aren't there."

"Jack, I feel very strongly about this. I have a theory. I think maybe one of Joseph's sisters had the baby and she used Joseph's identity. She would know Joseph's Social Security number, she would be within a few years of Joseph's age—"

"OK, it's a good theory to work on. But if you can't prove anything positive, DNA can prove the negative."

"Let's leave that for a last resort."

"OK, honey. I'll pick up Eddie and we'll go somewhere exciting for dinner."

"Like Pine Brook Road?"

"Sounds good to me."

"I'll call you later."

I hung up feeling better and worse, better about my family, worse about Joseph. I hated the thought of her being considered a suspect in a murder she could not and would not have committed, whether she was related to the victim or not. I looked at my watch, knowing that the chances of my returning home tonight were diminishing. It was really more important that I talk to Joseph's sisters than that I spend the night in my own home. Air travel was too expensive for me to contemplate yet another trip when this was done.

I had the sisters' names, addresses, and phone numbers in my notebook and I found them quickly. The first one was Betty McCall. I dialed the number.

A woman answered as though she were right next to the phone.

"Mrs. McCall?"

"Yes?"

"This is Chris Bennett. I'm a friend of your sister, Sister Joseph. Katherine."

"Oh, yes, hello. Where are you calling from?"

"I'm in the building of the insurance company your sister worked for some years ago when she took a leave from St. Stephen's."

"I know just where that is. Will you come and have a cup of coffee with me?"

"I'd love to."

She lived in a pretty, white, colonial-style house about twenty minutes from Fine and Houlihan. If I had to guess, I'd say she was fifty, give or take, which is about what Joseph is. She was wearing a dark pantsuit and tugging at the collar of a dog that desperately wanted to go out.

"How nice to see you, Chris. Are you afraid of wild animals?"

I laughed. "Not that one." I bent over and patted the dog, murmuring the kind of sweet nothings that seem dedicated to dogs and babies.

"I've got the coffee ready and I'll put this little trouble-maker out in the yard so we can have a little peace. You look just like what I expected."

"Did Joseph tell you about me?" I wondered if that was the name I should have used.

"We still call her Katherine and yes, she talked about you from the time you were a child and first went to visit the convent."

"She saved my life back in those days," I said truthfully.

"It seems to be her nature. It's hard to believe, growing up with Katherine, that she would have become the person she is now."

"Have you talked to her lately?" I asked, stepping gingerly into my unpleasant task.

"She called and said there was some problem that no one had to worry about but you might call. She said she'd given you my number and my sister's. I didn't expect you to fly to my front door."

"I had some other people to see," I said. "And it's much nicer to look at someone when you're asking questions."

"Milk? Sugar?"

"Just black, thank you."

There were slices of cake on a platter and tasting a crumb I realized it was gingerbread, a favorite of mine. When Betty had poured, we sipped our coffee and I took out my worn notebook. Needless to say, by the time I was ready to ask my first question, I liked her so much I couldn't imagine that she would ever have practiced the deception that I had suggested to Jack over the phone.

"I'm interested in the year, about twenty years ago

or so, when Joseph—Katherine—came back here on leave from the convent."

"I remember that quite well. She stayed in Mom and Dad's house which was on the other side of town from where the insurance company is."

"Where were you at that time?"

"I was already married. We hadn't bought this house yet. We lived in some nice garden apartments not too far from Mom."

"Did you see a lot of Katherine that year?"

"Oh, yes. We were over at Mom's a lot and she came to us—they all did—for Sunday dinner and we got together whenever we could."

"Did you have children at that time?" I asked.

"Let's see." She seemed to be counting years. "Yes, I had two. A boy and a girl. They're both out of college now and living on their own."

"You have another sister, I think?"

"That's Hope. She's close enough that I get to see her as much as I want."

"Where was she living that year?"

"Mmm. She'd had some health problems and she was still home with the folks."

"And that's where Katherine was living, too?"

"Yes. It was a wonderful house, a room for everyone. That house must be a hundred years old now." The thought made her pause.

"Was it Hope who stitched up skirts for Katherine to wear to work?"

"It must have been. She's always been a very talented seamstress. She can look at a picture of a dress and figure out how to make it. A real gift."

"Is she married now?"

"Oh, yes. Has a wonderful husband."

"Children?"

"Well, no. As I said, she had some problems and that kept her from having children. But she's active in the community and in the church and she's leading a very full life."

"She never adopted," I said, not looking at her.

"There was some talk, but no, they decided not to."

"Did she ever—have a miscarriage or anything like that?"

Betty shook her head. "She couldn't have them. That was about it."

I decided not to press it. I didn't want to tell her what the story involving Joseph was, since Joseph apparently hadn't told her herself.

"That year that Katherine was home, what kind of year was that? Was there anything memorable about it?"

"Memorable. My goodness, if there's one year in my life I'll never forget, it's that one. There's never been another year like it, to which I say, thank goodness."

17

I felt a surge of hope swell inside me. Perhaps I had finally hit on the right question, one that would yield productive answers. "Could you tell me about it?" I asked.

"Well, just having Katherine home for all that time was memorable. She lives so far away and we just don't get to see her all that often. And then there was B.G."

"B.G.?"

"He was a cousin on my father's side, Barton Gilbert Bailey. We called him B.G. from the time he was a little bit of a thing. He got sick and we knew it was bad. I'm sure that's why Katherine came home. She wanted to see him before he died. She thought maybe she could take care of him but that didn't work out. He needed more medical attention than she could give him. And he had a little boy. So we took Little B.—or rather, Mom and Dad did; I wasn't living there at that time—and B.G. went to the hospital. He did come back home once or twice, I think, but it didn't last. He died while Katherine was living here."

"Didn't he have a wife to help him?" I asked innocently.

"She was gone by then. Georgianne was one of those

155

women in the nineteen seventies who decided she'd had enough of life as a wife and mother and took off. You wouldn't remember, you're too young, but some women did that. Said they were sick and tired of staying home and doing useless things around the house and off they went somewhere else to do things they thought were useful. Most of them," Betty said with a hint of derision in her voice, "ended up running day care schools and things like that, taking care of other people's children instead of their own."

"Is that what she did?"

"That's exactly what she did. B.G. was well rid of her."

"What happened after he died?" I asked, purely out of curiosity. I couldn't imagine this had anything to do with what happened to Joseph.

"She never came back," Betty sighed. "She'd taken herself to California and she thought the weather there was just lovely, much nicer than we have in Ohio. She inherited the house, of course, because they never divorced and she sold it for a bundle, but she left Little B. with my parents, who sent him out to see her every summer at their expense."

"Where is Little B. now?"

"He's not far from here. I guess he's all mixed up on how he feels about his mother but he never went out to California to stay. He seems to take to Ohio weather better than she did."

"This is great gingerbread," I said, wanting to put an end to the turn the conversation had taken. Betty was clearly angry at her cousin's wife's behavior, and I couldn't blame her.

"Well, we all love it and it takes only a minute to bake. More coffee?"

"I'd love some."

She poured for both of us and then she heard the scratchings at the back door and left to let the dog in. "He's never satisfied," she said cheerfully. "But I guess he's had a good run. Maybe he'll lie down and rest after all that hard work." She leaned over and petted the dog affectionately.

"Was that what made the year so memorable," I asked, "Katherine coming home and your cousin dying?"

"That was also the year my brother disappeared."

"Disappeared?" I said.

"Well, I guess you'd say he ran away."

"Katherine said you had a brother and she didn't know where he was."

"Well, it all happened that year. Timmy was always trouble. Mom always said thank God she'd had three daughters and one son and not the other way around. Not that it always works that way. My son is an angel."

"So's mine," I said. "He's two and a half."

Betty laughed. "They're all angels at that age. Even Timmy was a doll when he was little. But in his teens he just kept getting into trouble. It was awful. Sometimes Katherine was able to help, but mostly it was one thing after another. When he left Ohio, we just didn't know where he was."

"You mean you've never heard from him in twenty years?"

"Oh, we've heard from him, but not very often. The last time must have been five years ago. I think he was in Canada then. He'd been in Mexico the time before."

"Was he living at home with your parents when he took off?"

"He had been, but then he got his own little place for a while."

"How did you find out he was gone?"

"He sent a letter to Mom and Dad. Said by the time they got it, he'd be gone. That was it. Mom cried for weeks. Then B.G. died and she cried some more. What a year. We can all do without one like that again."

"What did your brother do?"

"Oh, he worked at this and that, a mechanic in a garage, helping out in a Laundromat that his friend owned, things like that. He never had what you'd call a steady job. Mom always gave him money when he needed it so he didn't go hungry, and I guess he had enough to pay the rent when he moved out of the house."

I looked at my watch. I had to make a decision right away and cancel either the hotel room or my return flight. "Do you think I could talk to your sister?" I asked.

"I can call her for you."

"I'd appreciate that."

She went into the kitchen and came back with a cord-less phone. While she dialed I hoped I'd be lucky. She had said her sister was busy at community affairs, which meant she was likely to be out in the afternoon. "Hope? Hi, it's Betty."

Good, I thought. I listened while they exchanged sis-terly gossip. Then Betty asked if I could come over. She looked over at me. "She's free now. You could be there in twenty, thirty minutes."

"Fine."

She made the arrangements and I asked if I could call the airline. I assumed I'd be going back tomorrow but I asked if they would leave the ticket open. That done, Betty wrote directions to her sister's house and I was on my way.

Hope McHugh's house, which was occupied by two adults, was larger than her sister's and set on a larger piece of property. It was meticulously kept, the plantings absolutely exquisite. There was a three-car garage attached and I was led to wonder how two people could drive three cars, and gave up. I have learned that possessions have little to do with need once you get past the basics.

Mrs. McHugh opened the door at my ring, a melodious chime that went on and on, and it was clear that she was the great beauty in the family. Younger than Betty and probably a little younger than Joseph, she had the remnants of strawberry blond hair and skin to match.

"Chris?" she said with a welcoming smile.

"Hi."

"Please come in. Betty called a little while ago and my sister Katherine called the other day. She said you had questions for us."

I explained, without going into detail, that there was a problem and it seemed that events of that year Katherine was on leave were the key to what had happened.

"Well, I remember that year very well. It was the worst year of my life."

The entry hall of the house was a two-story atrium, natural light streaming from above and a magnificent chandelier that could provide its own light when the sun was down. Straight ahead at the back of the house was a beautiful room that we sat down in, the windows looking out on the grounds and a pool that would have had my Eddie running for his bathing trunks. We are a family of swimmers. I told her how beautiful it all was and then took out my notebook and pen.

"You've really come prepared," she said.

"I've talked to several people and it's important to preserve what they told me."

"I'd love to have you work on one of my projects."

"I understand you're involved in charitable work."

"It's what I do. We raise funds for the hospital, for the church, for babies with HIV. It keeps me busy and it's God's work."

"That's wonderful," I said, meaning it. "About that year . . ."

"That was the year Timmy left, the year Katherine came back, the year B.G. died. God, I haven't thought about B.G. for such a long time. How can it be twenty years?" Her eyes glistened with tears.

"I understand you were ill yourself that year."

"Yes, I guess so. When trouble hits, it just doesn't seem to stop."

"What made you ill?"

"It was—it was my reproductive system. It left me unable to have children."

"Were you hospitalized?" I asked.

"For a few days."

"Which hospital?"

"Good Samaritan. It's a Catholic hospital near here. It's where B.G. died." She looked at me, her eyes full. She attempted a smile. "You sure have dredged up an awful lot of painful memories in a very short time."

"I apologize for that, Hope. I really do. It's just that it may be important."

"I understand."

"You've never been pregnant, then? Never had a miscarriage?" I wanted to know how far she would go with the truth I was looking for.

"No. Never." It was a whisper. "They gave me a hysterectomy."

"In your twenties?" I sounded as horrified as I felt.

"It was twenty years ago. It's what they did then. Things have changed a lot. You can use drugs today where at that time they didn't exist."

"I'm sorry for your trouble," I said.

"It was a long time ago. I've led a very lucky life since then. I have a wonderful husband and I devote my time to doing what I think is good."

"It is good. Let me ask you something else. Katherine said someone made skirts for her to wear to work. Was that you?"

"Yes, it was. She came home with only her brown habits and she needed some secular clothes to wear at her job. She didn't want anything fancy so I stitched up some skirts in a couple of different colors and she got blouses to go with them." She said it as though it were the easiest thing in the world.

"You must be very talented," I said.

"Some people can put cookies together. I put skirts and dresses together. It's just something I'm able to do."

I looked down at my notebook. "Have you had any dealings with God's Love Adoptions in Cincinnati?" I watched her face carefully as I asked the question.

"I've heard of them, but I don't recall ever talking to anyone there." Her face had not changed. If the name had come as a shock, she didn't show it.

"A Mrs. DelBello?"

"I don't think I know anyone by that name."

"Did you visit Good Samaritan Hospital during the year that Katherine was home?"

"I'm sure I did. I visited B.G."

"Did you go with Katherine?"

"Maybe once or twice, but I preferred not to."

"Really? Why?"

"I think Katherine liked it better if she went alone."

That was interesting. "I understand his son, Little B., came to live with your family."

"He did. There was that awful business with B.G.'s wife leaving and someone had to take care of him. It fell on my mother. Everything seems to have fallen on my mother," she said lightly. "Mom was a magician. She could handle anything, which was good because she had to handle everything. She was really something else."

"I gather you were living at home the year that Katherine was there."

"Yes, except for a couple of months when a friend of mine from school needed a roommate for her apartment in Cincinnati. I begged my parents to let me stay with her just till her lease ran out. I never thought they'd give permission, but they did. It made it easier for them once they had Little B. with them. It was a big house but it wasn't that big!"

"Do you remember what months you lived in the apartment?"

"Spring, I think. Maybe into the summer."

May is a spring month. May was when Randy Collins was born. "Does that friend of yours still live around here?"

"Yes. She's married and they have a house. Why?"

"Would you mind if I talked to her?"

Her face clouded over. "Could you tell me what this is about?"

"I can't, Hope. It's about Katherine and I can't talk about it till we find out exactly what happened."

"But if it's about Katherine, how can my friend have anything to do with it?"

"I can't explain. But I think Katherine would want you to give me her name and address."

She shook her head. "This is about me, not Katherine. What do you think I did, living in that apartment? And what difference does it make?"

"I don't know what you did. I just know it's important that I speak to your friend."

She wavered, sitting on the sofa with both hands palms down on the cushions, as though ready to move, but not quite decided whether she should or not. "I'll give it to you," she said, "but only because Katherine called and said I should try to help." She got up and left the room, returning a minute later with a square of paper on which was written a name, address, and phone number. "Her name is Mary Short now. You can probably get her at home around dinnertime. Is there anything else?"

"I'm sorry to have upset you. There is one other thing. I'd like to talk to Little B."

"No one calls him that anymore except family. He's Bart now. He's married. I can give you that number, too. Is that all?"

I got up and followed her to the atrium and waited there while she went to a room beyond the dining room. She came back with another square of paper. I thanked her and apologized again for upsetting her, but she didn't smile. She was clearly distressed and I thought she might call Joseph tonight and ask what all this was about. Joseph would probably guess what I was after. If she chose to tell her sister, that was her business. I was glad to have gotten the information I now had in my notebook and on the two squares of paper. There was more work to do.

18

I drove to the hotel, checked in, then called Jack and brought him up to date. Then I called Mary Short who invited me to come over this evening. Before I went downstairs to have dinner, I called Bart Bailey and talked to his wife. Bart hadn't come home from work yet but he would be there around six or so and then they would have dinner. I told her I wanted to talk to him and she said they weren't going anywhere tonight, so it was still possible I could see him after I spoke to Mary Short.

As I ate dinner in the hotel restaurant, I thought about Hope McHugh as the possible mother of Randy Collins. Suppose Hope had cut her hair short. In fact, I had no idea whether she wore it short or long twenty years ago. I had seen no old pictures in her house. Suppose she didn't wear makeup. Suppose she wore the kinds of skirts and blouses she had run up for Joseph to wear to work. And why not? If she could make them for her sister, she could make them for herself. She could have easily installed a phone in the apartment she shared with Mary Short in the name of Katherine Bailey. No one asked for identification when you got a telephone. You put down a deposit and paid your bills. When I moved into Aunt Meg's house, I had the name changed on the bill with no trouble at all. In fact, I noticed that the bills that came to the house were addressed to Uncle Will, who had died many years before. As long as the bills were paid, nobody cared.

The more I thought about it, the more plausible it became. Hope had lived in the same house with Joseph for much of the year that Joseph was here. She could easily have looked in Joseph's bag, found her Social Security number, if she needed it for the adoption agency, and any other documents she might have required. I wished I could have seen the hospital file but I knew I couldn't get access to that without a court order—or the way Randy Collins had, by getting a job at the hospital and looking at it herself.

When I finished my dinner, I went upstairs, grabbed my coat since it was a chilly evening, checked at the desk on how to get to the Shorts', and took off.

"I've known Hope forever," Mary said as we sat in her living room. In a nearby room, where her husband was sitting by himself, a television set was making a constant noise.

Mary Short was tall, something of a contradiction, and wore jeans and a cotton sweater adorned with a beautiful silver pendant on a black cord.

"Hope told me you shared an apartment for a few months about twenty years ago."

"That's right. It was a lot of fun, the only time I ever lived in my own place. I had a job in Cincinnati and I roomed with someone else for a while and then my roommate announced she was getting married and she moved out a couple of weeks later, leaving me with a rent bill I couldn't manage."

"And a lease you couldn't get out of," I volunteered.

"That, too. So I called Hope and she asked her parents and they said since it was me, she could do it. She was old enough to do what she wanted, but she was a good daughter."

"She's a lovely person," I said. "Do you remember if she had her own phone when she shared that apartment with you?"

Mary pressed three fingers against her lips, thinking. "I think she had one put in after the first month. I had a boyfriend—it was my future husband—and we talked incessantly. Hope couldn't even call home without asking me to get off." Mary rolled her eyes and laughed. "Now I scream at my daughter for doing the same thing."

"How was her health during the time you lived together?"

"Hope had problems. It was very sad. She was in pain, she missed work sometimes, she saw doctors. I can't say she was in good health, but she never lost her spirit."

"How did she wear her hair?" I asked.

"We all had it long for a while. It was the style. Then we both went out and cut it short. We looked much better and the sink stayed a lot cleaner." She laughed again.

"Was it short while she lived with you?"

"We cut it while we lived together. I remember that."

"Did she leave the apartment for any period of time?"

"She went back to her parents' sometimes on the weekend."

"That's all?"

"That's all I remember."

"Mary, I'm going to ask you something that may shock you but I'd appreciate an honest answer. Did Hope ever give birth to a baby?"

"No. Hope? No. No. Why would you ask such a thing?"

"It's important. Did she ever look pregnant?"

"Never. No."

"What happened when the lease expired?"

"I got married."

"And moved out?"

"Yes."

"What happened to Hope?"

She looked very serious now, the sparkle in her eyes gone. "I think she moved out, too. I'm not sure. Why are you asking these questions? What would ever make you think that Hope—she can't even have children. They gave her a hysterectomy. It was the end for her. She's never really gotten over it."

"Did you ever see her phone bills?" I asked. "Did you ever see the envelopes they came in?"

She shook her head, clearly bewildered. "I don't know. Maybe. She usually came home first, I think. I don't know." She looked confused, as though wondering where these strange questions were leading.

"I just wondered if the phone bill was in her name."

"Who else's name could it have been in? Her parents didn't pay for it."

"Did Hope have a boyfriend while you lived together?"

"Hope always had boyfriends," she said without stopping to think. "She may have met her husband during that time. The truth is, I was in love and I was self-centered enough to think about very little except myself. If I'd been a better roommate, I wouldn't've hogged the phone the way I did."

"What's her husband like?"

"He's wonderful. Kind, devoted, rich, although that came a little later. He adores her. I couldn't imagine her marrying anyone better. And he knew when he married her that there would be no children."

"I'm a little surprised that they didn't adopt a child."

"That was their decision. They didn't want to."

"I don't have anything else to ask you," I said. "I appreciate your candor."

"I wish I understood what you were after."

"It's complicated and I'm not at liberty to say any more than I have."

She showed me to the phone and I called Barton Bailey's number. Bart was home and would be happy to see me.

The Baileys were a nice young couple, both of them younger than I. They lived in a small house with a one-car garage and one car outside in the driveway. The three of us sat in the living room, Wendy slightly apart from us in a comfortable chair.

"My cousin Katherine called and said I might hear from you," he said, looking at me warmly. He was much too tall to be called Little anything but I noticed his wife called him B. I stuck to Bart.

"She's been busy calling," I said. "I'm trying to get some facts together and I can't tell you much about why. I just hope you'll be forthright."

"It's my middle name," he said with a grin, and I noticed Wendy smiled, too.

"Do you remember the year your father died?"

"Oh, yeah. I still think of it as the worst year of my life."

"Katherine came home that year. I'm told she came because your dad was sick."

"At the time, I had no idea why she was back. But at some point I think I realized that's why she came. That was a long time after. Everybody loved my father. I couldn't exaggerate that. His death left such a big hole in the family, they still haven't recovered."

"That's the way your cousins talk about him," I said.

"And he and Katherine were special friends."

The phone rang and Wendy got up and went to the kitchen. When she answered, she pushed the door shut.

"She said as much to me," I said.

"I brought down some albums when I heard you were coming. You interested in family pictures?"

"I'd love to see them."

He sat next to me on the sofa and opened one large, fat album that started with black-and-white pictures. "That's Dad when he was three," he said. He pointed out his grandparents, his father as he grew older, the cousins Katherine, Hope, Betty, and Tim where they appeared. There were a lot of pictures of B.G. and Katherine together, one with his arm around her as they sat on the ground with a picnic basket nearby.

Color pictures started to appear. B.G. was there with a number of girls. "That's my mom," Bart said pointing to one. "That's around the time they met."

"She was a good-looking girl," I said. The girl in question had a great smile, a lot of hair, a very thin figure. "But you look like your dad."

"I know. I don't know what happened between them. She up and moved out one day. Dad always said, 'People change.' I kept wondering why, but I never got an answer. She just didn't want to live here anymore, didn't want to be his wife, didn't want to be my mother."

"It must have been very hard for you."

"It still is," he said, his voice wavering.

We went back to the pictures. He turned a page and I saw Joseph wearing the habit of a novice. "Oh!" I said with pleasure and surprise.

"Yeah, there she is when she decided to become a nun."

"Was that after your dad married?" I asked.

"It must have been. There are some pictures somewhere of her graduating from college. That's when she decided to become a nun. If you figure out the years, Dad was married by then." He pulled over a smaller album and began to leaf through it. "See? Here's Katherine graduating. And there she is in the habit."

The pictures were carefully dated and he was right; she had graduated first and become a novice afterward. The album was on my lap. I turned a page, then another. It wasn't a very large book but I saw that it contained only pictures of Katherine and B.G. I didn't say anything, just kept turning the pages. There were several blank ones at the end. B.G. had died before filling them. The last pictures were from the year Katherine had come home. She was wearing secular clothes, something I had never seen, but her face looked very much as it had the first time I had met her, when I was thirteen or fourteen and visited the convent. These had not been taken very long before my first visit.

"Seen enough?" he asked as I stared at the last page.

I said, "Yes," with my heart pounding.

"They had what you'd call a special relationship. For

my father it lasted forever. They never got as close as my mom and dad did, but they never got as far apart either."

"They were cousins," I said softly, feeling an incredible pain. "I have a cousin I'm very close to."

"I think I've told you everything," he said.

"Yes." I could hardly find my voice. "I think you have." I handed him the small album, almost reluctant to let it go. "It's late for me to be up. I should be getting back to the hotel."

He took my hand and held it. "I'm glad you came. I haven't looked at those pictures for a long time."

His wife came out of the kitchen just as I had buttoned my coat. I wished them both well.

Back at the hotel I called Jack and told him much of what I had learned. The older sister, Betty, I had ruled out completely as the mother of Randy Collins. But Hope was a definite possibility, in spite of the fact that her roommate denied she had ever been pregnant. I told him a bit of my conversation with Little B., but not all of it.

"Doesn't sound like he added much," Jack said.

"Not so far as who gave birth to Randy."

"Any chance it could have been Sister Joseph?"

I gave what must have sounded like a moan. "I can't rule it out, but it's very unlikely."

"But who would have been the father?" Jack asked. "She took a leave to be with a sick cousin, she got a full-time job. You can't tell me she had an affair with someone she met at work. I may not know her as well as you but I can tell you she's not the kind of woman who'd bed down with a guy she met on the job."

"She isn't, and she didn't. At this moment, the sister's the best possibility. She even had a phone in her own name and her roommate had one in hers."

"So she could have listed herself as Katherine Bailey."

"Right."

"Maybe I can trace the number for you."

"The phone number? After twenty years?"

"Just a maybe. Let me see what I can do. And I have a suggestion. Your idea that Randy's mother could be one of Sister Joseph's sisters is a very good one. Have you thought that maybe it could have been someone at work? Someone who knew she was a nun and would be going back?"

"It crossed my mind. Maybe I'll go back to Fine and Houlihan tomorrow morning. Then with luck I can get on the same plane I didn't take tonight."

"I think it's worth your while asking."

"How's my little sweetheart? Did he ask for me?"

"Nah. We had a guy evening, good dinner, coupla beers. Your name never came up."

"I love you, too," I said, stifling a giggle.

19

It was a good suggestion to follow up on. From the size of Fine and Houlihan, there could have been several people working in the clerical and administrative parts of the business. I had seen a number of people at computers when I walked from reception to Mr. Fine's office. Twenty years ago those computers would have been typewriters and maybe there would have been fewer of them, but there was certainly the possibility that two or three other people had worked in the area when Joseph was there. And no doubt they all knew each other, talked to each other, probably even lunched together.

I took a shower and curled up on the bed with a couple of pillows behind me, my notebook on my lap. If Hope McHugh had been Randy's mother, what did that tell me about who had murdered Randy? Nothing, I thought. The idea that Hope had found out that Randy was at my house and had come to Oakwood from Ohio was so preposterous, so incredible, I put it out of my mind. The only way that Randy's natural mother might be her killer was to believe that the mother knew who Randy was, where she was living, and had followed her to Oakwood with a gun intending to threaten Randy or do harm to her. Eventually, even if it were possible, it was beyond the limits of probability, not to mention the fact that murdering one's child was inconceivable to me.

But Detective Joe Fox could make a good case that Joseph was both the mother and the killer. As he would see it, Joseph would be so concerned with her position as Superior of St. Stephen's that she would do anything to protect herself from exposure of the truth. And he could concoct a scenario in which Randy had spoken to Joseph and told her of their purported relationship, after which Joseph had come down to Oakwood Sunday morning and killed Randy. Perhaps he would even decide that I was the carrier of the information. If he checked my phone bill, he would find a long call to St. Stephen's, the one I had made to Grace. In his mind, that could have been a call to Joseph. All calls were routed through the switchboard so there was no record of who had been the final person to pick up. And since the nuns had refused to cooperate with him, he had no reason to believe that Grace was the person I had spoken to.

None of these ideas gave me much hope. I got up in the morning thinking the same thoughts that had been running through my mind as I fell asleep the night before. After breakfast, I optimistically checked out, put my bag in the trunk of my little car, and drove to Fine and Houlihan.

"I'm sorry, Mr. Fine is out of the office today," the receptionist said when I came in.

"Is Mr. Houlihan here?"

"He is but—" She looked at her watch. "Let me see if he has time for you."

Apparently he did because she led me through the

center work area to an office the size and shape of his partner's, but at the other end of the row.

"Miss Bennett, is it?" Jerry Houlihan asked expansively. He was one of those good-looking Irishmen with an enviable head of white hair, very blue eyes, and a wonderfully warm smile. He could probably sell me anything if I stayed with him long enough.

I shook his hand and started to tell him about my visit with his partner yesterday, but he interrupted me.

"I know all about it. Abe and I had a chitchat before we went home last night. It was Katherine Bailey you were asking about, is that right?"

"Yes, it was."

"Lovely young lady. They don't make 'em better than that. You know she was a nun?"

"I'm a friend of hers, Mr. Houlihan. I've known her for a long time."

"Wonderful girl. What can I tell you about her?"

"Actually, I wanted to ask about other young women who worked in this office at the same time as Katherine."

"You're out to tax my memory, I see."

"Maybe there are records you could check. Maybe there's someone in the office from—"

He was shaking a finger at me. "I never forget a face. I never forget an employee. Tell me what you're looking for."

"Women who worked here at the same time as Katherine. Maybe someone who quit while she was here, maybe someone who was pregnant, maybe someone who became ill and couldn't work."

"In the year that Katherine Bailey was here."

"Yes."

He dropped his head forward and closed his eyes. I

had the sense of a human information retrieval system at work. He took a pencil and wrote on a sheet of paper in front of him. When he came out of his reverie, he picked up the phone and pressed a button. "You wanna come in here, Myra? I've got a little job for you."

A woman in her thirties, nicely dressed but not looking like a New York executive secretary, appeared at the door a second later.

Houlihan handed her the sheet of paper. "Try looking for these names in the old file. They worked here maybe twenty years ago."

Myra took the paper and left without a word. Jerry Houlihan offered me coffee and went to get it himself. We talked a few sips' worth when he came back and then Myra turned up with the files.

"Good girl," he said appreciatively and with a distinct lack of sensitivity that seemed to go right by Myra. "Here we go. Carla Higgins. I remember Carla. Nice girl, nice looking. Worked here for a while, left for a while, came back, stayed a couple of years, then left forever. Want to have a look?"

I reached over for the folder, hoping there might be a picture of her, but there wasn't. "What did she look like?" I asked.

"Tiny little thing, petite, you'd probably say. Five feet tall if she stretched. Cute as a button."

"Do you recall why she left?"

"She found a job that paid better somewhere, didn't like it, and came back to our happy family."

I smiled. He was a bit of a character. I flipped through the file but found nothing that would make her a possible mother for Randy Collins. If she was only five feet tall, Mrs. DelBello would have remembered her size. "Do you know if this address is current?" I asked.

"I'd have to guess that it isn't, but that's where she was living last time she set foot in our office."

I jotted down the address although I didn't intend to visit there unless she turned out to be the most likely of the prospects and I had time to spare.

He took the folder and handed me a second one. "Ginny Forster. I loved that girl but she couldn't spell 'the.' She was everybody's friend. If you needed an aspirin, Ginny had one for you. If you cut your finger, she had a Band-Aid. I think she used to fix up some of the girls with old boyfriends of hers—not Katherine, of course, but the others. A heart as big as an elephant."

I listened to the description with enjoyment and looked at her file. Like the previous one, it told me nothing relevant to the birth of Randy Collins. "What did she look like?" I asked.

"Oh, medium height, I'd say, medium hair, not too dark, not too light, pleasant, outgoing, slim, a smile that made you feel good. If she could've spelled, I might've married her myself, except, of course, I was already married to the most wonderful woman in the world."

"I see she left in April of that year," I said.

"Sometime in the spring, that's what I remember."

"Do you remember why?"

"One of those boyfriends panned out, I guess. She decided to get married and he didn't want her to work. Kind of outdated outlook, but who am I to criticize the young?"

"She was still slim when she left?" I asked.

"Never changed, that Ginny. What a lovely girl."

I wrote down the address. Her married name had

been added, perhaps because they had to send her tax statements the following year. I handed back the folder and waited.

"And here's the one you've been waiting for." He gave me a big grin and handed the third folder to me. "Barbara Sawyer. She worked here for a couple of years, got herself pregnant, came crying to me about it, asked if she could stay on. A lot of places wouldn't have let her, you know, but Abe and I talked about it and decided what the hell. It was better that she work as long as she could than go on welfare. So she stayed till she was bulging and then she left. She even came back afterward."

"Did she keep the baby?" I asked.

"Now, that's a good question. She didn't come back here for maybe six months so I kind of assumed she was home being a mother. But when she started working again, she didn't talk about the baby at all and we didn't ask out of politeness. She got married eventually; that's her address right there on the first page. Haven't seen her for a while but as far as I know, she's still married, has a couple of kids, and I think she's got herself a nice life."

"I'd like to talk to her," I said.

"I wish I could figure out what you're after." He looked at me with a face that said: Tell me.

"I really can't discuss it," I said. "I'm sorry. This is between Katherine and me."

"Well, then I won't push. You take the address and phone number and maybe Barbara'll talk to you. Her married name is there, too, right under Sawyer."

I found it and wrote it down, "Phillips." I looked at my watch and decided I'd better get going. I wanted very much to make that plane this afternoon and get back to Jack and Eddie.

Before I left, Mr. Houlihan called the number for Barbara Phillips, talked to her, and said I would be coming within the half hour. Then I dashed.

It was a small house with a basketball hoop at the side of the driveway. The woman who opened the door was in her forties, wore little makeup, and had on jeans and a red man-tailored shirt. The shirt was the only bright thing about her. She had a sallow complexion and her hair was faded, strands of gray visible throughout. We were about the same height so she fit the description Mrs. DelBello had given me.

We sat in her living room and I took a deep breath before beginning. "I want to ask you some questions about a painful time in your life, Mrs. Phillips."

"What do you mean, painful?"

"You gave birth to a child about twenty years ago."

"Oh my God."

"I'm not going to spread this around, but I need to know about it for the sake of someone else."

"How did you find out?"

"Mr. Houlihan told me. I asked if anyone worked in the office that year who might have been pregnant."

"It was a long time ago. I haven't talked to anyone about it for years."

"Where did you have the baby, Mrs. Phillips?"

"In the hospital. Good Samaritan."

"Did you keep her?"

"Her? I had a boy."

I could have kicked myself for being so stupid, for

asking a question that assumed something I didn't know. "What?" I said.

"I had a boy, not a girl."

"Did you keep him?"

"No. I gave him up. I was single—I guess you know that already. My mother couldn't help out and I couldn't work if I had to take care of a baby."

"What adoption agency did you use?"

"Uh, I had a lawyer handle it. I didn't go to an agency."

"Do you know who adopted your baby?"

"We decided to keep the whole thing quiet, anonymous. The lawyer has the name, but I never saw it. They came from out of state is what I remember."

"Have you ever heard from your child?"

"No, never."

"Have you made any effort to find him?"

"No." She looked sad and troubled. "Why do you need to know this?"

"It's very complicated. It has to do with an adopted child that was born twenty years ago at Good Samaritan Hospital. I don't think it was your child, but I want to get as many facts as I can. Did you see your baby before you gave him away?"

"They brought him to me, yes. I held him. He was real cute, had a lot of dark hair. He was probably the best looking of all my children."

"Who brought you the papers to sign?"

"Oh, I don't know. I guess it was the lawyer or someone who worked for the lawyer."

"A woman?"

"It could've been a woman."

"You remember her name?"

"No."

"Mrs. DelBello?"

She thought about it. "I don't remember that name."

"Would you give me your lawyer's name?"

She looked at me, then away. "No, I won't give you his name. I don't want to answer any more questions. And I don't want you talking to people about this. I want my privacy. Jerry Houlihan should've known better. It wasn't anybody's business what happened to me."

"I know and you're right. Thank you very much. I appreciate your help."

I got in the car and drove away as fast as I could. I was aware that Barbara Phillips was watching from the front window, the curtain pulled back as I started the motor. I felt a little ill. I was inquiring into things I had no right to know and I was hurting the people I was talking to, just by asking my questions. Maybe Barbara Phillips had really given birth to a girl and had decided to lie to me just to screw up my facts. I wouldn't blame her. I knew she would now think about this, whether she wanted to or not, this unhappy chapter of her past that she had believed was set aside.

I had hurt Hope McHugh, too, and I felt terrible about it. When Joseph heard about my inquisition of her sister, she would be justifiably angry, even if she understood my motives.

At a traffic light I tried to think of what else there was to accomplish before I went home. I couldn't think of anything so on the green I found my way to the airport, returned the car, and got myself on the next plane to New York.

So what had I accomplished in these two days? I asked myself as I flew east. I had two possible suspects for the mother of Randy Collins: Hope McHugh who swore she had never been pregnant, and Barbara Phillips who swore she had given birth to a boy. As I sat watching the heavens go by, I reviewed my conversation with Barbara Phillips. So much of what she had said might be untrue. I had stupidly tipped my hand by asking about the baby as though I knew it was a girl and she might have just decided to foul me up, to confuse me in order to get rid of me. It hadn't occurred to me until now, but what if she thought I was an agent for the child? Maybe I was trying to set up a meeting between them, a meeting that the child wanted and that she wanted no part in. I could see now I had handled it very badly. But that meant she might well be Randy's natural mother. The dates worked out and that was the most important thing, not to mention the fact that she had actually given birth. But I could think of no way to prove she was the mother unless a court ordered a blood test.

Thinking further, I had to wonder if there was any way she could have been involved in Randy's death, and I could see none. She was a wife and the mother of teenagers. To imagine her in Oakwood last Sunday morning with a gun was beyond the limits of my imagination.

But if she was the mother, Joseph wasn't, and that was what I was out to prove. Eventually, it all put me to sleep.

20

Jack and I arrived home at about the same time. Eddie's absolute glee at seeing me raised my spirits to the roof. I think my greatest reservation about leaving a small child is that you can't fully explain that you will return, that he shouldn't worry, that Mommy will absolutely come back. I spent a lot of time with him that evening, happy that the weekend was upon us and I would be around for the next two days. When he was finally exhausted, I took him upstairs and put him to bed.

"You're getting too big for a crib, Eddie," I said. "Would you like a bed to sleep in?"

"Wanna bed."

"Let's go shopping for a bed soon. Maybe we can get it for your next birthday."

He was too tired to respond. I kissed him and put a light blanket on him. He was asleep before I left the room.

"Lots going on," Jack said. He had gone out and bought a pizza with everything possible on it, since neither one of us was up to cooking dinner. It smelled wonderful and we sat down to eat it, Jack sprinkling hot pepper flakes on his, as though the pepperoni wasn't quite spicy enough for him.

"You first, then. Almost everything I have is a maybe."

"The bad news is Joe Fox is getting antsy. It's almost a week since Randy Collins was murdered and he's got less than you have. He's pushing hard for Sister Joseph to take a DNA test—give blood for it—and Arnold will have none of it."

"I'm with Arnold. If Joseph says she's not Randy's natural mother, she isn't."

"Most of the world doesn't share your assurance, dear wife."

I leaned over and gave him a kiss.

"Yech," he said. "Olive oil and mozzarella all over my face."

"Keep talking."

"And there's the question of where Sister Joseph was last Sunday morning. I told you, Father Kramer says she wasn't at mass."

"Then she was somewhere else at mass."

"I'm sure any sane judge in New York State will accept your opinion as fact."

"Jack, I don't think people should have to expose their private lives because a cop can't find a killer."

"Spoken like a true libertarian, but not very realistic. I have a feeling if she doesn't acquiesce in the next couple of days, Fox is going to get a court order for a blood sample."

"Arnold will explode," I said.

"Maybe, but I think the court will grant it."

I chewed up the last of my pizza slice and took a long drink of Coke, into which I had squeezed a wedge of lemon. "You said that was the bad news. What's the good news?"

"The good news is that you're home."

My heart sank. "That's it?"

"Hey, I'm walking on air. So's Eddie. You're home. What could be better?"

"What am I going to do?" I said. "All I have is faint possibilities that someone else may have given birth to Randy. No admissions. Both women deny it emphatically."

"Start from the beginning."

I did. I went over the whole twenty-four-hours-plus that I spent in Ohio: including the visit to Mrs. DelBello; then to Abraham Fine at the insurance office; to Joseph's sisters, Betty McCall and Hope McHugh; and then to Little B.

"Sounds interesting, her relationship with her cousin."

"I have a close relationship with a first cousin, too."

"Not exactly the same thing."

"It was obviously a close family," I said. "The sisters are close and the cousin was close. When B.G. went to the hospital, Joseph's mother took in his young son."

"So you've ruled out Betty McCall."

"She was married and had two children the year that Joseph was home."

"Very unlikely she gave birth and no one noticed it."

"Very."

"But the other sister is a possible."

"Definitely, which doesn't mean she's the one. Her roommate swears she wasn't pregnant."

"And who else?"

I told him about my second visit to Fine and Houlihan just this morning and the three leads Jerry Houlihan had given me. The last thing on my list was my visit to Barbara Phillips.

"Let me get this straight," Jack said. "This is a woman

who worked in the insurance office at the same time as Sister Joseph."

"Right."

"And while she was working there—this other woman—she got pregnant and left to have the baby."

"Right."

"Looks good to me."

"She says she had a boy."

"That's a detail. I'll bet she also told you she didn't use the adoption agency that Randy came from."

"She said she had a lawyer."

"You get the name?"

"She wouldn't give it to me."

"It's a nice circumstantial case. She mention the hospital she gave birth in?"

"She did before I started digging. It's the same hospital."

"Lotta action in that hospital," Jack said. "Chris, you looked at these women. Any of them look like they could be related to Randy?"

"If you mean was one of them an older version of Randy, the answer is no. They all have medium to light coloring. Barbara Phillips had a washed-out look to her. Her hair seemed faded and there were strands of gray. Hope McHugh is probably the lightest of the bunch. Randy was fair. All of them are on the slim side. Barbara Phillips could have looked inside Joseph's handbag when Joseph was in someone's office and gotten a look at her driver's license, birthdate, that kind of thing. And Hope was living at home most of the year that Joseph was there. So the same goes for her." I took a deep breath. "It's hard when you sit across from someone to imagine her being so duplicitous."

"That's why we try to keep our distance, figuratively, at least. The problem is, it's so circumstantial, I don't see a judge requiring either of those women to submit to a blood test, especially if Sister Joseph doesn't submit to one."

"So there we are. And pushing it one step further, I don't see either of those women in Ohio flying to New York, buying a gun, coming to Oakwood, and shooting Randy. It's almost silly when you think about it."

"Then maybe there's no connection between who Randy's mother is and who killed her."

"That's what I think."

"Unless Sister Joseph is the mother."

"She isn't," I said firmly.

There was a little pizza left to freeze for another day and I wrapped it in foil while Jack did the dishes. "Questions still unanswered," I said. "Did Randy steal our ax? Did she chop down the Greiners' tree? If she did, why on earth did she? And if she did, is it possible that someone in the Greiners' house saw her do it and came out mad and shot her?"

"It's possible," Jack said easily. "But where did the killer get the gun?"

"I guess he could have stolen it from Mr. Kovak."

"That makes sense."

"Go prove it," I said. "Mr. Kovak says the gun was stolen but there's no record that he reported it. His wife used to leave the back door open while she was out and lots of people knew it, including the Greiners. One of the Greiner kids could have gone in and taken it. But I'm just ranting and raving. I don't want to find out that a killer lives on our street, still I desperately want to find the killer for Joseph's sake."

"What you've got to do now is let Sister Joseph know what you've got and let her take it from there. I'd bet she won't be too keen on picking her sister as Randy's mother, but she has to be told what you know."

"There are two more people I'd like to talk to. I don't look forward to this, but maybe something will come out of it."

"Who's that?"

"Randy's parents."

"Not a bad idea."

"Maybe they know something about her that will turn me in a new direction."

"I'll call Joe Fox and get their address. Better still, why don't we call Arnold? I'd rather deal with him about this than Joe Fox."

"I couldn't agree with you more."

I called Joseph first. Like the other nuns, she usually goes to bed fairly early, although her work often keeps her up later. She sounded unruffled, exactly like herself, which made me feel good. She told me about her meeting with Arnold this morning, the things they had discussed, none of which had anything to do with Randy Collins.

"I couldn't ask for a better advocate," she said. "He remembers everything I've said, asks all the right questions, knows the law, and is very comforting."

"That's all true, but we've got to find out who killed Randy or you're going to have a difficult time."

"I know that. And I've heard from my sister Hope."

"She wasn't very happy," I said.

"I told her you had to ask her all those questions and

not to worry about it. I appreciate your not mentioning the reasons for your asking."

"I wouldn't do that. It's up to you to tell people what you want them to know. Do you recall that Hope lived in an apartment for part of the year that you were back home?"

"She mentioned that you asked about that. Are you thinking she gave birth to Randy during the time she lived there?"

"It's a possibility."

"It didn't happen, Chris. My poor Hope. She wanted so much to have a baby of her own and they gave her a hysterectomy. You can't imagine how sad that made her, made all of us. If she had had a child, she would never have given it away."

"There's another candidate," I said. "A woman who worked at Fine and Houlihan when you were there."

"You think one of those people could have used my name?"

"Why not? Who would ever know? She looks in your bag and finds your Social Security number, your driver's license number, your birthday."

"That's a very interesting idea. There was a pregnant woman at that office."

"Barbara Sawyer," I said.

"Barbara, yes. And she wasn't married. I'm sure she knew I was a nun. They all knew."

"The problem is, I don't see any way of getting her to give a blood specimen to check it out."

"Yes, that would be quite awkward. Is she married?"

"Yes, and has two children."

"Did she admit she'd had a child that year?"

"She said it was a boy, but I asked the question badly. She gave birth at Good Samaritan."

"I think we should put this in Arnold's capable hands."

"I'm going to call him, Joseph. I need some information from him. Do you want me to tell him everything I learned?"

"Please do."

"You sound very good," I said.

"I have no reason not to feel good. I'm innocent of everything and I have an excellent lawyer. Not to mention my personal private investigator."

"I'll keep you posted," I said.

"So, you've been traveling." Arnold sounded elated.

"I couldn't see any way to do it from home and the first person I wanted to talk to said it would be easier for her if I came to her house."

"Hey, it's always easier if someone gets on a plane and flies to where you are. Very generous of you."

"I've learned a lot, Arnold."

"What a surprise. Let me in on it."

I went through it all again, listening to his approving comments and answering his occasional questions.

"It sounds like you have two candidates—and they're good candidates—for the mother of the deceased."

"But I don't see any way to prove that either one of them is or isn't Randy's mother."

"That's for me to worry about. You've done the legwork and you've got lots to show for it. I think you can relax now, or is that asking too much?"

"Much too much. I'm really calling to ask you for information."

"That's a switch. Let's hear it."

"I'd like to interview Randy Collins's parents. Do you have their address?"

"I do."

"Have you spoken to them?"

"No, but it's not a bad idea. Let me get it for you."

He left the phone, came back, and gave me their names and address. They lived in New York State, about halfway between New York City and Albany, so their daughter wasn't far from home when she went to college, but just far enough that she needed to live on campus. I could drive there in a few hours, which meant I could be back on the same day. I was relieved I didn't have to go back to Ohio, where they had adopted Randy. And even more relieved that they hadn't migrated west.

I got their phone number from information, got my courage up, and dialed.

21

The arrangement I made with the Collinses was that I would drive up on Sunday afternoon and talk to them. It was Mr. Collins who answered the phone. When he heard who I was, that his daughter had been staying with me at the time of her murder, he was very anxious to get together with me. He and his wife had numerous questions about their daughter's activities during her last few days and they knew I could fill them in on much of what had gone on.

During the conversation, he left the phone a couple of times to consult with his wife, but she never came to the phone herself. I could hear voices and assumed there were people visiting, making a condolence call for the worst of bereavements.

When the conversation was finally over, I sat with Jack and told him what I had arranged. "I'll take Eddie with me," I said. "I'd rather not leave him so soon after I disappeared on him."

"I'll drive you up," Jack said.

"Oh, Jack, that's such—"

"No sweat. We'll all go up together and I'll stay in the car with Eddie while you're talking to them. You won't be there more than an hour."

"I wouldn't think so."

"I'll whip up something for dinner tomorrow and there'll be enough for Sunday, too."

"Are you sure you can take the time?"

"It's Sunday. I passed the bar. I didn't bring any work home with me. I'm a free man."

So that was how we left it. Saturday was a quiet, calm day. Eddie and I went shopping for food, running into Mel as we drove down Pine Brook Road on the way home. After I had put my purchases in the refrigerator, Eddie and I went back down the street to Mel's house and we sat in the backyard, Mel and I gabbing, Eddie playing with Sari and Noah.

"I haven't heard a word of scuttlebutt," Mel said. "The police have been up and down the block, interviewing everyone who lives here. I doubt whether anyone knows anything about that poor girl's death. It didn't exactly happen at high noon."

I told her I was going to talk to Randy's parents tomorrow.

"What can they tell you? She hadn't been home for a long time."

"But she kept in touch. Maybe she said something to them that will give me a lead. I'm sure Detective Fox has talked to them. I want to know what they know."

"They must be in pretty bad shape."

"I'm sure they are. I don't look forward to this, Mel. When I was in Ohio, I had the feeling I was leaving a trail of disaster everywhere I went. I was lucky not to get a dart in my back."

"You're gutsy, Chris. I don't know if I could do it."

"Tell me about the Greiner boys," I said. "You live next door to them. What are they like?"

"One's OK, the other's a little trouble."

"How so?"

"The older one. I hear him coming home at all hours, not every night, but weekends."

"Anything worse than that?"

"I've heard whispers. I hate to repeat things like that. He may have had a couple of run-ins with the police. What are you thinking of?"

"I'm wondering if someone who knew that the Kovaks leave their back door unlocked could have gone in and picked up the gun."

"I thought of that myself," Mel admitted. "It's funny. The people who live here the longest are still the most trusting, although they complain the most about how the town has changed for the worse."

"The Kovaks have lived here a long time. They said when they came, there was no reason to lock your doors. My aunt lived here even longer but I can't remember what she did. I would come down, run over to Greenwillow and visit Gene, then have dinner and go to sleep. I didn't have keys and locks on my mind. But if a neighbor had stolen the gun, then maybe came home so late that Randy was already up and walking down the street with an ax—"

"And if he'd had something to drink," Mel added.

"It might add up to accidental death."

"I don't know how you're going to get the police to search the Greiners' house. They'll need a warrant and Hal says you can't just tell a judge you think maybe you'll find a gun somewhere in that house if you just let me go through it."

"That sounds like what Jack says. I don't know, Mel.

A girl is dead, a tree is cut down, a gun is missing, and nobody has any answers."

Mel gave me her famous grin. "But you, my dear friend, are on the way. You're thinking right. And that'll get you there."

I just wondered where "there" would turn out to be.

We drove upstate after mass on Sunday. About noon, we stopped for lunch. Eddie was delighted with the booster seat they brought for him and he ate well. Once Jack grabbed Eddie's milk glass just as it was about to tip and I went through a pack of napkins keeping the face and the environment reasonably clean and dry. For the most part, Eddie was a good camper.

We had only a short distance to drive to the Collinses' house and in the time it took to get there, Eddie fell asleep. Jack had brought a book to read so he was set. I leaned over and gave him a little kiss as I gathered my bag and notebook and got out of the car, pushing the door closed quietly so as not to disturb my sleeping child.

The front door to the house was opened by a forty-something man, probably closer to fifty, wearing a tie-less shirt and slacks. We shook hands and introduced ourselves and went into a pleasant room with a skylight at the end of the house. Mrs. Collins was there wearing a black pantsuit, a slim woman with dark hair turning tastefully blond. But if ever a face showed its owner's feelings, hers did. She looked totally washed out, her eyes almost too heavy to stay open. I expressed my condolences and told both of them that it had been a pleasure meeting their daughter and having her as my guest.

As I had expected, they had at least as many questions to ask me as I had to ask them. I let them begin, answering with almost everything I knew. I had no intention of spreading Joseph's story if I could avoid it.

When I had told them what they wanted to know, I opened my notebook and began to ask my own questions. They told me that Randy wanted to work in New York City for the summer and that she was looking for a job. That was to make money. Her other objective was to locate her birth mother, a goal she had been pursuing for a couple of years.

"How did she go about it?" I asked.

"We told her the name of the agency through which we had adopted her," her mother said. "It's in Cincinnati. We had lived in Ohio and we remembered the name of the woman who had worked with us at the agency. A couple of summers ago, Randy went out there and visited cousins of ours and met that woman."

"Mrs. DelBello," I said.

"That's the one. How did you know?"

"Randy told me. What did she do after she met Mrs. DelBello?"

"She spent the summer there, didn't she, Bob?"

"She got a job. This Mrs. DelBello gave her a small lead. I think she told Randy what hospital she'd been born in."

"And then?"

Mrs. Collins smiled. "She was a very determined girl, very persistent. I think she managed to make friends with a nurse or a nursing student to try to get information."

"It didn't work," Bob Collins said. "She came home at the end of the summer very disappointed. But she got herself a job at that hospital the next summer, using our cousins' address as her own."

"So they would think she was a local girl looking for a summer job," I said.

"That's right. And it worked. They hired her to do something or other, not very exciting work but she didn't care. It gave her the access she needed, and she went back and spent the summer working there."

"How did you two feel about her spending all this time and effort on her search?" I asked.

"She knew we loved her," her mother said in a voice that was a whisper.

I waited while she gathered herself together.

"This was something she wanted to know. We had no objections. After all, we know who we're descended from, what allergies they have and what things they love and hate. She had every right to know those things, too." She stopped and looked at her husband.

He picked up the cue and continued. "We assisted her when she needed help, but the truth is, she didn't need much. She was a very bright girl. She did well in school and when there was something she wanted to learn, she did the research, went to the library, used the computer. But she always knew she had our backing."

"What did she learn that summer at the hospital?" I asked.

"I guess she had time on her hands—or she made time—while she worked. She went down to the old records room and found the file on her birth. The name of her birth mother was either in that file or she was able to find it by cross-referencing. These were paper documents, you understand. Twenty years ago, hospitals weren't using computers the way they do today."

They looked at each other. "She didn't give us a name," Mrs. Collins said. "But she told us it had turned out to be someone living in New York State, someone connected with a convent."

"St. Stephen's Convent," her husband said. "It's not too far from here."

"I'm familiar with it. Go on."

Mrs. Collins drank from a glass of water on the table beside her. "There was a nun she was going to talk to but first she wanted to see an ex-nun."

"I'm the ex-nun," I said.

They looked at me in surprise. "Then Randy found the ex-nun," Mrs. Collins said. "Finally. Finally we're getting some answers."

"Do you know how she found me?" I asked.

"She probably asked around," Bob Collins said. "I told you. She was good at digging up facts. Maybe she stopped off at the convent at some point."

Obviously Randy hadn't let her parents know where she was those last days of her life and I wasn't going to tell them things that would distress them. "Did she call you in the days before she died?" I asked.

"Not every day," her father said, "but frequently enough that we didn't worry."

"Did she tell you she had found her birth mother?"

"Not exactly. I'm pretty sure she knew who this woman was but she kept it to herself."

"She arrived at my house on Thursday and asked if she could stay," I said. "Later, she told me she was leaving on Sunday. Sunday morning her body was found down the street. Did she tell you what she was going to do on Sunday? Where she was going? Whether she might be meeting someone?"

"It was a little jumbled," her father said. "But she said she was meeting someone from the convent on Sunday morning."

I felt a wave of cold pass through me. "Did she give you a name, Mr. Collins?"

"She was very excited and it all came out in a long monologue that was hard to get straight. There was the nun and the ex-nun. If she was staying with you, then it must have been the nun that she was going to meet."

"I want to ask you about something entirely separate from all this," I said. I didn't want to hear any more that would get Joseph into trouble. "Randy was found lying near a tree that had been cut down and it appears she may have cut it down herself. Does that sound like something Randy would have done?"

"She loved trees," Mrs. Collins said. "What a strange thing, Randy cutting down a tree. It seems crazy. She loved trees and flowers."

"We'll find the reason, Mrs. Collins," I said, "if it turns out to be true."

"It can't be true," her mother whispered. "She was such a good girl."

"Let me ask you a question," her husband said, emphasizing the "you." "When Randy was found, she was wearing strange clothes. Do you know anything about that?"

I hadn't wanted to talk about it but he had put me on the spot. "When she rang my doorbell, she was wearing the habit of a Franciscan novice."

They both nearly exploded. "Why would she do that?" Mrs. Collins said, her voice strong.

"She had been at St. Stephen's. She had apparently taken the habit from the laundry room."

"But why?"

"I think she felt that I would be sympathetic to a novice, since I'd been connected with the convent for many years. Otherwise, she was just a girl out of the blue standing on my doorstep."

"This is so strange," Mrs. Collins said.

"Did she wear it the whole time she was with you?" Bob Collins asked.

"Yes, she did. It was only after her death that we found out she hadn't been a novice and she hadn't had any connection with the convent. But we learned she had visited there. She had been friendly with one of the novices, a girl about Randy's age."

"And do you think this is all connected with her search for her birth mother?"

"I'm sure of it. That was the only information she wanted from me. But she was very conflicted, I can tell you that. I think she was afraid to confront the person she thought might be her birth mother."

"Was this nun going to help her?"

"I'm not sure." I hoped he would drop it right there. One thing I would not do is say anything about Joseph, including her name.

"So what we now know," he said, summing up our exchange of information, "is that she took a habit from the convent, went to your house, spent a couple of days with you, and made an appointment to see a nun from that convent on Sunday morning. I think I'm more confused now than when you came in, Miss Bennett."

I had the same feeling. "But we all know a little more and maybe that will help us find the answers."

"How did Randy get from Albany or from the convent to your house?" Mrs. Collins asked.

"She told me she had come by train, which is a long trip and requires changes, and that she took a cab from the Oakwood station. But when I checked at the station, no one had any record of driving her to my house."

"That doesn't mean anything," Bob Collins said. "They probably just drove her off the books, you know, no record of a fare, no tax to pay."

"That's possible. And maybe that's what happened."

We all sat there for a few moments, trying to think our way through what we had learned. I looked at my watch. "I'm going to leave now. I appreciate your help and your kindness."

Bob Collins stood. "Please let us know if you find out anything else. I think I'll call that detective and tell him about the connection with the convent."

"He knows about it," I said.

"So he's just not talking, at least not to us."

"I think he wants to be careful not to implicate an innocent person in a terrible crime."

He seemed to accept that. I really didn't want him telling Detective Fox I had been up here to see them, but if he did, I would live with it. At the door, I gave him my name and phone number and he grasped my hand warmly. I was in tears as I left him.

22

Eddie was still asleep in the backseat so we talked as Jack drove us home.

"They think Randy had an appointment with a nun last Sunday morning?" he said, skepticism apparent in his voice.

"Yes. I don't know what to do about this."

"You can be pretty sure Joe Fox knows about it," Jack said. "If he's talked to them, he's asked a lot of the same questions you have."

"Which is why Joseph is a suspect. He thinks she had an appointment with Randy and she won't account for her time Sunday morning."

"So where could she have been that she wouldn't want to talk about?"

"I don't know, Jack." I heard my voice rise with fear and frustration. "I'm sorry. I'm not yelling at you."

"I know that, honey. But let's think. Could she be involved in some alternative kind of church that she goes to sometimes?"

"Joseph doesn't get involved in stupidity," I said.

"How about this? Could she have met one of her sisters that morning? Maybe she drove down to New York

City, went to church down there, and had breakfast with her sister?"

"This is very scary."

"But it's possible. She could be protecting her sister."

"But her sister couldn't have known about Randy, about Randy being at our house, any of this."

"Maybe Mrs. DelBello made a phone call."

It was possible. She could have called "Katherine Bailey" after she heard from Randy Collins. But that was almost two years ago, and there were so many other things that didn't fit. "Why that weekend? I didn't talk to the sisters till after Randy had been shot."

"Maybe Sister Joseph and Randy had already talked by the time Randy came to Oakwood." He said it quietly, an offering that I had no wish to sample.

"Joseph didn't lie to me."

"You sometimes withhold truths for what you consider good reasons."

"Joseph didn't kill Randy. Joseph didn't give birth to Randy."

"But maybe her sister did, on both counts."

"And if Randy had already spoken to Joseph, why did she come to see me?"

I looked out the window. On any other day I would have enjoyed this drive. I would have loved looking at the scenery. I would have been happy to be spending time with my husband and son on a sunny Sunday afternoon in May. But on this day I was distraught. I couldn't believe that Joseph had done any of the things that the evidence seemed to point to. But I wasn't the detective. I wasn't the jury that would hear the apparent evidence. I wasn't the judge who would charge the jury.

Jack reached out and patted my arm. "We'll get to the bottom of this," he said.

"How much should I tell Arnold?"

"Tell Arnold everything. If anyone in this world is more skeptical than you about what looks like damning evidence against Sister Joseph, he's the guy. I agree with you, Chris. She didn't give birth to Randy and she didn't kill her. There are still things we don't know. I know it looks as though you've exhausted all your leads, but you haven't. And before you ask me how I know that, I'll tell you that since we both agree that Sister Joseph didn't do either act one or act two, there's still something we don't know."

"You always manage to make me feel better," I said.

"That's why there are two of us."

There was a message on our answering machine from Joseph when we got home, just a brief sentence that I should call her. It made me uncomfortable. What could have happened that would make her call?

"You're getting paranoid," Jack said when I told him how I felt.

"I hope you're right. I'd rather have it in my head than in reality."

"Pick up the phone and call her. Maybe she's inviting you to tea."

"You are a dreamer. I thought you were the realist in this union."

"Don't give up on me. When you least expect it, I'll be back to realism. You'll wish I were still a dreamer."

I gave him a hug, knowing it was true. Then I dialed St. Stephen's.

"Chris," Joseph said when we were finally connected, "thank you for getting back to me. I didn't mean to interfere with your Sunday."

"We were upstate. I talked to Randy Collins's parents."

"Those poor people."

"Yes. How are you doing?"

"I got a call from my sister Hope this morning. She's made a decision that will interest you."

"Oh?"

"She's decided to have a blood test, to check her DNA. She's very distressed and wants to prove to you that she's not related to anyone you think might be her natural child."

"I see."

"I tried to talk her out of it. I don't think people should have to prove their innocence, especially in a case like this when I know she had nothing to do with Randy's birth or death. But she's adamant. She said she hasn't felt right since she spoke to you and to her friend Mary Short, and while she's sure her husband believes her—and I certainly believe her—she wants to prove scientifically that she's not involved in this affair."

"Have you told Arnold?" I asked.

"Yes. I called him at home."

"Is she giving her blood tomorrow?"

"Yes. As soon as she can. I believe getting a complete DNA analysis takes a long time, but some things can be ruled out very quickly. She might be the wrong blood type and they would know that quite soon."

"So we may know in a couple of days which way it's going."

"That's right. I just wanted you to know. Did you learn anything from the Collinses?"

"Nothing that makes me happy."

Joseph laughed lightly. "Out with it," she said. "Did Randy tell them that I was her birth mother?"

"No, she didn't. But they knew there was a connection with St. Stephen's. I didn't tell them everything I knew but I acknowledged that she had been there and had befriended a novice. What she told them is that she had a meeting with a nun last Sunday morning."

"Oh my. I suppose we can expect that Detective Fox knows this."

"I'm sure of it. He's spoken with them."

"Chris, I never met—"

"Joseph," I said, interrupting, "I don't want to hear this. I believe you. I have never doubted you. I will never doubt you."

"Thank God for good friends," she said.

"Amen."

Eddie had awakened from his nap before we had reached home, and after being belted into the car seat for a long time, he was hard to keep down. We took a walk and ran into an acquaintance of his with her mother. The four of us stood around, the mothers talking, the children rolling around on the grass and giggling. When they grew tired of each other, we moved on.

It was a beautiful day followed by a warm evening. After Eddie was settled in his crib, Jack and I sat outside. We had taken the summer furniture out only recently and it was good to use it.

"I guess this new development means that Hope isn't Randy's mother," I said.

"I would think so. She'd hardly submit to a test if she were."

"So that narrows down my suspects. If it's the woman who worked in the insurance office, I'll never find out. I wish I'd taken pictures of those women to show Mrs. DelBello."

"You could get a picture of Sister Joseph to her."

I looked at him. "So she could rule it out."

"Why not?"

I thought about it. "I couldn't do that without her permission. And I'm not sure she'd give it. And any picture I could send would be in her habit, which is not the way Mrs. DelBello would remember her."

"The family probably has old ones."

I felt myself getting tense. There were lots of old pictures in Little B.'s album but I didn't want to put Joseph's life in the hands of someone who might make an error, whose real vision as well as her recalled vision could have deteriorated in twenty years.

"You don't want to do it, do you?" Jack said.

"No." I got up and walked around, looking at the new green shoots in the garden. It was my favorite season and my enjoyment had been curtailed by this mess. "I want to find Randy's mother, her birth mother. And I want to find her killer. I don't care if it's the same person or two different people. I just don't want to put Joseph on the spot."

"Well, let's kick it around a little. You're convinced that whoever gave birth to Randy Collins knew Sister Joseph and used her identity."

"It has to be. If it wasn't Joseph herself, it was someone who knew her."

"Then this blood test that Hope is taking may help your case. If she comes up a possible mother, then her sisters would be possible mothers, too. Maybe you should give more attention to the sister who was married and had two kids already."

"It's mind-boggling. I just don't see how she could be the one. Let's wait and see what happens before I try to make that case."

"You know, I'm impressed with Randy Collins. She must have been a pretty smart cookie. Think about what she accomplished. She got Mrs. DelBello to give her just enough information that she could pick it up and run with it. She got herself a job at the hospital where she was born and figured out how to find the right files and dig out the right information. She sounds like a real treasure."

"You're right. I could have hired her to help me out on some of those homicides. She must have found me in some file at St. Stephen's. I can't think how else she would have come to me."

"So how did she do it?" Jack asked.

"There's a lot of trust at St. Stephen's, Jack. The nuns don't lock their doors and everyone respects everyone else's privacy. If you want to talk to someone, you knock and she calls you in. I've never really thought about it, but I don't think Joseph locks the door to her office either."

"Is that where the records are kept?"

"Not all of them, but most. There are others. Angela has a file in the telephone room. She can look up anyone's address or phone number in a minute. If a nun got sick, Angela would be able to find a sister's or brother's or niece's phone number just like that."

"Any secrets in her file?"

"I doubt it. What secrets would a nun have? If she had a boyfriend somewhere, she wouldn't be a nun anymore, not if that fact were in someone's file."

"What do you suppose is in the file Sister Joseph keeps on you?"

I had never thought about it. I had never sat with Joseph while she had a file on me open in front of her although I had no doubt that one existed. When I entered St. Stephen's, my aunt presented the convent with the required dowry. There was a record of that along with the amount I had been allowed to take out in order to buy a car so I could travel to Oakwood once a month to visit Aunt Meg and Gene. When I left for good, the remainder of my dowry was returned to me. So all of that would be in my file. What else? Perhaps any behavior problems that I exhibited as a young girl, perhaps my sadness at being separated from my family. If any student of mine or her parents complained about me or commended me, that would be included, too.

I told these things to Jack. "I'm sure my license number was recorded somewhere, too. I went to the doctor from time to time. I wouldn't be surprised if there's a record of that."

"So it's possible that by the time Randy landed on our doorstep she knew a little something about you."

"If that was of any interest to her. I can't imagine why she would want to know if I had an ear infection at the age of sixteen."

"But she might have known that Sister Joseph was your spiritual director while you were a nun."

"I would think so, yes."

"And maybe if she spent one long night going through those files she could have found out the names of the novices, what classes they were taking, and that sort of stuff."

"So she knew where to go to meet Tina. It wasn't a lucky accident."

"Nothing was an accident in that girl's life," Jack said. "Except getting killed. Where was Tina last Sunday?"

"She was home with her parents. Joseph spoke to her. She came back to St. Stephen's after Randy was dead."

"You see what I'm driving at? You've got a trusting bunch of women who wouldn't turn a hair if they saw a novice walk down the hall, even if they couldn't see her face. If it was a man, you'd hear from them. So if Randy was careful, she could get around. If she spent most of one night in Sister Joseph's office, could she get back into the dorm before daylight?"

"No. It's locked. But she could go to the chapel and kneel with her head down."

"Then that's what she did. And she not only searched your file and Tina's file, you can bet she went through Sister Joseph's as well. She knew that Sister Joseph had been in Ohio the year Randy was born. So Randy now knew it from two sources, the hospital file and the convent's."

It made a lot of sense. She had prepared herself well, going so far as to steal Tina's handbag in case she had to show ID somewhere. It had convinced me when I found it. "You know," I said, "I wrote a long letter to Joseph from here about a week after I left the convent. I kind of poured out my heart."

"And she kept the letter. Probably put it in your file folder."

"So Randy knew a lot about me when I opened the front door and saw her standing there."

"The question is," Jack said, "what else did she know?"

23

I thought I would have a few days in limbo starting with Monday until the results of Hope McHugh's blood test came through, but I was mistaken. Just before Eddie's lunchtime, while we were out front pulling up new weeds among the shrubs along the house, I saw a police car drive up Pine Brook Road and stop in front of the Greiners' house.

It wasn't that unusual to see a police car as our department is very helpful and cooperative. If you decide to take a vacation, they'll send an officer over to fill out a form telling where you'll be, how you can be reached, and what lights will go on in the evenings. But I wasn't the only one who found this one interesting. Several neighbors stepped out of their houses to see what was happening. Mr. Kovak was one.

"Peece car," Eddie said, pointing.

"Yes, that's a police car."

"Wanna see the peece car."

"It's lunchtime, Eddie. We'll see it later."

He stood and watched as the officer got out, put his hat on, and walked up to the front door, carrying something under one arm. Carol Greiner opened the door and nearly pulled him inside. I told Eddie to pick up the trowel he had been using and we carried the tools to the garage, then went inside for lunch.

The police car was there for about twenty minutes. While Eddie ate, I went to the front of the house a couple of times to check. The last time I looked, the officer came out the front door, stood on the step, and talked to Carol for a minute before returning to his car. He sat inside it and I couldn't really see what he was doing. Finally, he left.

I was consumed by curiosity. The Greiners' house was far enough away from ours that I could not see in detail what had happened. It had looked like Carol opening the door. I was pretty sure I knew which officer it had been, but I would not have sworn to it. He still had something pressed between his arm and his body as he left, but I had no idea what it was. When he opened the car door, he leaned in, probably dropping it on the seat next to his, before he got in himself.

And then nothing happened. I took Eddie upstairs for his nap and I went downstairs, hoping to hear something. I went out and did a little more work in the soil. Midge MacDonald came by, my neighbor on the other side of the house, and I got to my feet and walked to the street to talk to her.

"I hear the police were at the Greiners'," she said.

"One officer around lunchtime."

"Did he make an arrest?"

"Not while I was looking. He left the house alone, got in his car, and drove away."

"You think the police would tell me anything if I called?"

"I'm sure they wouldn't," I said. "But if you hear

anything, I'm just as eager as you are to know what's going on."

She walked on and I went back to my digging. Finally I went inside and called Jack.

"I think something's up," I said.

"Here, too. Arnold called me."

"Uh-oh. What happened?"

"The court has ordered Sister Joseph to take a blood test. Arnold said he'd appeal, but she said not to bother. She's going through with it."

"I see." I could tell from the ripple of fear that passed through me that something inside still worried that she might be related to Randy. I was angry at myself for feeling that way.

"You said something was up," Jack reminded me.

"A cop went to see Carol Greiner around noon."

"Interesting."

"Midge MacDonald came by and asked if I knew anything, which I didn't."

"So you want Sergeant Brooks to use his influence and find out what's going on." I could hear the tease in his voice.

"You got it, Sergeant."

"Well, why not? I haven't talked to anyone there for a while. Maybe they'll tell me something."

I sat with the paper and waited. Maybe I had made too much of a quick visit by a police officer. Maybe the Greiners were just planning a vacation or had a problem with a security alarm.

Jack didn't call back for half an hour and when the phone rang, I jumped. "I think things are starting to happen," he said.

"Tell me."

"I talked to the guy who's been my buddy since I moved in. Just asked him casually if there were any developments in the homicide. He said Carol Greiner had called the station house this morning and said she'd just found something that she wanted to turn over to the police. They sent a guy over and he brought back a gun."

I drew my breath in, feeling elation. "*The* gun?"

"Well, he says the serial number matches the one on Kovak's gun and his permit file paperwork."

"Fantastic," I said.

"Don't jump on it just yet. It'll take a coupla days till they can compare it with the murder weapon. But your theory about one of the Greiner boys stealing the gun looks pretty good right now. My guy says Carol Greiner found it in one of her sons' bedrooms."

"Poor Carol," I said. "She must really be going through hell."

"That's what the cop said. He was very sympathetic about the family, said these things happen and it's really tragic."

"I assume what you've told me is to go no farther."

"I'd keep it under my hat for a while. In a couple of days, when they finish the ballistics tests, they'll make an announcement one way or the other. Oh, and by the way, they did some digging and found the missing report on Kovak's lost gun."

"So he was telling the truth."

"Looks like it. Not all obnoxious people are liars."

"And not all tree lovers are immune from family problems."

"Right. Something to think about. I've got another nugget for you."

"About what?"

"I called my contact at the phone company last week about that number for Katherine Bailey in the Cincinnati area about twenty years ago. He got back to me a little while ago. You want the number?"

"You bet." I wrote down the number and street address as he read it. "I'll call Joseph and ask her if she recognizes it."

"He said the number wasn't assigned to Katherine Bailey for very long, less than a year. It was cancelled a month or so after Randy was born."

"So the woman established it before she went to God's Love and got rid of it when her dealings with them were over."

"It sure looks like you're right on that. Well, we'll know soon."

"Maybe," I said.

"What does that mean?"

"Just what I said."

I called Joseph next. She told me what Jack had, that she had decided it wasn't worth appealing the decision requiring her to give blood. It had been a matter of principle and she didn't want to waste Arnold's time. She had already given a small sample and that was that.

Although I knew I shouldn't repeat what Jack had told me about the discovery of the gun, I told her and asked her not to say anything till something definitive was announced.

"It still doesn't make sense," she said. "Would a teenage boy kill a girl who was chopping down his mother's tree?"

"We'll find out. I have something else for you to think about. Jack dug up the telephone number assigned to Katherine Bailey during the year you spent in Ohio."

"So there actually was someone with my name who had a phone?"

"Yes, and not for very long. About a month after Randy's birth, the phone was disconnected." I read her the number and address.

She waited several seconds before she said, "The address means nothing to me. Maybe the number is familiar. I'm not sure. I'll think about it. It's just possible that I have an old address book somewhere. Maybe that would help. I know it's not my mother's number. Both my sisters have changed their numbers but I can't tell you when. Whenever they moved, I suppose."

"Just think about it. If it's in your memory, it'll work its way out."

"Everything else has in the last few days, not all of it happy."

"I know. But I think we're going to get some answers soon."

"Did you hear the Greiners had a gun?" It was Mel, calling after school.

"How do you know that?"

"Someone across the street saw the police come this morning. She's pretty sure he had a gun in a plastic bag when he left. Everyone at school is buzzing about it."

No wonder, I thought, it was impossible to keep secrets in government. "Well, I'm glad you know because I was told not to say a word."

"Is it the Kovak gun?"

"That's what I've heard."

"So he was telling the truth. Isn't that amazing?"

"So far everyone's been telling the truth. I'm sure Carol had no knowledge that that gun was in her house."

"Carol wouldn't touch a gun," Mel said. "She hates them. What else do you know?"

"Not much. When they do the ballistics tests, we'll find out if that's the murder weapon."

"I can't believe this whole thing is going to be solved because a woman cleaned up her house and found a gun lying around."

"I hope no one in her family did it," I said.

"Me, too. They're my next-door neighbors."

Later that afternoon, in as quiet and subdued a manner as they could muster, the Oakwood police arrested the Greiners' older son. I was happy to see that they did not handcuff him. Carol looked terrible, her face stained with tears. She held her son's arm until he got in the back of the police car. Her husband looked grim and drove himself and his wife in his car.

A number of people stood around watching. I stayed on our front lawn but I scanned the group to see who was there. The Kovaks were not, which I thought was very kind of them.

Midge MacDonald walked by on her way home. "I hope that's the end of it," she said. "But I can't believe that boy did it."

"I can't either."

"He looks like such a child. I hope Carol doesn't collapse."

"So do I."

"See you."

I waved and she moved on.

Tuesday was such an ordinary day I was almost able to believe that there had been no homicide, no question about the birth of Randy Collins, no blood tests, no missing gun. In the morning I went to the college. In the afternoon I put my house in shape and took Eddie out shopping with me. But when he wasn't asking me questions or clamoring for my attention, I wondered about the phone number. I thought about the results of the blood tests. And I kept asking myself whether Randy had found something in Joseph's file that had somehow foreshadowed her death.

24

On Wednesday things started humming. Jack called to say that the Kovak gun was confirmed not to be the murder weapon.

"I don't understand," I said.

"It's the same caliber, thirty-eight, and could have fired the same type of ammunition, but it didn't fire the bullet that killed Randy. All the test firings and comparisons rule it out."

I said, "Whew. That means the Greiner boy is off the hook."

"Off the hook for homicide but he's facing some pretty serious felony charges, any one of which could mean prison time."

"Maybe they'll go easy on him," I said. "I'm sure after all this he's learned a lifetime lesson."

"It's possible. His lawyer may try for a 'YO'— youthful offender treatment and probation. I'm glad to hear you're still the optimist I married."

"But we don't have a killer and we don't have a murder weapon."

"Be patient. We should start to hear preliminary reports on the blood tests soon, especially if they're negative."

"I can't wait."

*   *   *

He was right about the blood tests. In the afternoon Arnold called.

"I've just talked to my client and given her the news and she said I could tell you, too. Sister Joseph is absolutely excluded as a possible parent of the homicide victim."

"Arnold, that's wonderful."

"There was never any doubt that this was pure harassment."

"But it's a relief. I assume she's no longer a suspect."

"There isn't a chance in hell that they'll pursue this. I want that detective to give her an apology."

"It's probably not in his nature," I said. "And I suspect it doesn't matter to Joseph. She always knew she wasn't related to Randy in life or in death. Now she can get back to her work without the distractions of the last couple of weeks."

"You have more sweetness and light in you than I have in me."

"You have other fine qualities, Arnold," I said with a laugh. "I assume Joseph's sister has also been excluded. That means my last suspect may be the—"

"Slow down, slow down. Who said anything about excluding the sister?"

"I just thought—"

"She hasn't been excluded. We won't know for a while about her. DNA takes a while to be processed."

"So it's still possible Hope is the mother?"

"Still possible."

I hung up with those words ringing in my ears. Still possible. It wasn't what I had expected.

Joseph called a little while later. "Chris, there are some

things I'd like to talk to you about. Do you think you could manage to come up here tomorrow?"

"Sure."

"I know it's short notice—"

"I'll come up first thing in the morning."

I decided to leave Eddie with Elsie and at nine-thirty I was on my way. I was at the convent well before lunch and immediately ushered to the office upstairs. Joseph was at her desk as I stepped inside.

"Chris, come in. It's such a beautiful day, we should be walking outside to talk, but I want to tell you a number of things and I don't want to keep you. This affair has already occupied too many people's valuable time. I don't know how I'll ever repay Arnold Gold."

"Just remain his friend," I said. "I think he values that so much that he couldn't measure it in billable hours."

She smiled at that and left her desk to join me at the long table where we customarily sat to discuss the various homicides I have worked on over the last few years. I took the seat opposite her, wondering what the purpose of this meeting was.

"When we first talked about Randy's death and how I might have figured in her life, I told you the truth about myself but I withheld some facts that I have decided to tell you now."

"Joseph, I don't think you should feel that I need to know any more than you've already told me. You're innocent of both charges. That's really enough for me."

"Let me be the judge of what you should know. Some facts may emerge that are going to look rather strange and may point—again—to the wrong person as the mother of Randy Collins."

"You certainly have my attention."

"While I have been excluded as a blood relative of Randy, my sister Hope has not. As sisters we should have the same genetic history. Siblings have the same set of parents while mothers and their children do not."

"I understand that. When cancer patients require matching bone marrow, they go to siblings rather than parents or children."

"Hope and I are not blood sisters."

"I see." For a bombshell, it was dropped rather delicately.

"I was adopted as a baby and brought up as a Bailey. I am a Bailey. I have never had the least interest in finding my birth mother and I doubt I ever will. When I was old enough to impress my family with the seriousness of my feelings, I said I did not want anyone outside the immediate family to know that I was adopted, that I felt totally part of the family, that I *was* part of the family. I have never told anyone until this minute that I was not born into the Bailey family. Not even Arnold," she added. "Although I suppose he'll deduce that now."

I sat thinking about the implications of what she had just said. When Arnold had told me yesterday that Joseph was excluded as Randy's mother but Hope was not, I had felt confused. With this new information, yesterday's facts were no longer confusing. In terms of blood, the two women weren't related. They had totally different genetic makeup. Nothing in their DNA would be similar.

"Then either of your sisters is still potentially a candidate for Randy's mother," I said.

"From a biological point of view, yes, they are potentially candidates. From the point of view of people that I have known all my life, they aren't."

"But Hope hasn't been excluded."

"That's right. And they may not be able to exclude her, even if they can't say definitively that she is Randy's mother. And the same would be true, I suppose, if Betty submitted to a test, which I don't want her to do."

She stopped and I knew I was meant to draw a conclusion. "There was another sibling," I said finally. "I forgot."

"Yes." She pulled a sheet of paper toward her. There was writing on it, illegible in the upside-down position from which I saw it. "I sat with this phone number you gave me for a long time last night. Numbers are such funny things. At some point in your life your Social Security number becomes engraved in your brain. You could probably wake up after being unconscious for days and be able to repeat it. There are phone numbers I remember from my childhood and others that I forgot as soon as I heard them. How many years ago did we begin to learn zip codes? And why can't I ever remember anyone's but my own?" She smiled and looked at the sheet of paper in front of her.

"I was sure I knew this number but I just couldn't attach it to a person. I went through a box of old papers of mine and couldn't find an address book that went back twenty years. So I called my sister Betty."

"It was hers?"

"No. But she recognized it after a minute. She said, 'Katherine, that was Timmy's number after he moved out of Mom's house.' "

"Your brother," I said. "The mother of Randy wasn't in your family; the father was."

"It appears that way. As I thought about it last night, it occurred to me that that may have been the real reason he moved out. He may have had a girlfriend that we didn't know about—I can tell you we knew nothing of Timmy's girlfriend—and when she became pregnant, he must have gotten the apartment for them to live in." She thought for a moment. "Or perhaps she already had an apartment and he just moved in with her."

"And when she decided to give up the baby, she got a phone in your name in that apartment."

"I can't tell you that this little story is true, Chris, but it certainly explains the facts we have."

"It does. I've just been chasing down a mother and we come up with a father. I would guess your brother didn't marry the mother of his child, or they wouldn't have given her away."

"I don't know, but that sounds reasonable. I asked Betty for the last known address or phone number she had for him and this is what she gave me." She handed me a half sheet of paper with Tim Bailey's address in Canada on it. "I don't know if he's still there. It's not a new address."

"If you don't mind, I'll try to run him down."

"I wish you would. It certainly explains why we haven't seen him in so many years. He had to know about this. Had to be the source of the information on me. He's probably ashamed of what he did. I'd just like to see him again."

I folded the paper and tucked it in my bag. "What I'm thinking is that neither your brother nor Randy's birth mother could have had anything to do with her death. Randy was trying to figure out how to approach you.

I'm sure she had no idea that someone had stolen your identity."

"You're right. And that means we still don't know who killed Randy."

"Or why."

There was a knock on the door and our lunch trays were delivered. I was glad of the break. What I had to ask Joseph next made me feel uncomfortable.

We talked about other things as we ate. Harold, the groundsman, was being obstreperous about something, which was par for Harold. Registration at the college was up for September's class, a happy occurrence. Joseph had done some traveling in the past year to encourage young women to apply and it had paid off. And the nuns in the Villa had drawn a diagram of their proposed vegetable garden and couldn't wait to plant their tomato and eggplant seedlings.

When we finished and Joseph had poured coffee and we had eaten our dessert, I decided the time had come. "Jack and I have been talking," I said. "We were both quite sure that whoever Randy's mother was, she wasn't responsible for Randy's death. Jack believes that Randy came into your office one night when everyone was asleep and spent a lot of time going through your files." I glanced over to the large metal cabinets she kept along the wall behind where I was sitting.

"That's possible. I sometimes work late in here but once I go to bed, I don't come back till after breakfast."

"And no one else comes in."

"They have no reason to."

"When Randy came to our house, she knew I was your friend. Do you think she could have found that out from a file you have with my name on it?"

"I would think she could reasonably deduce it."

"We think she may have learned information on other people from your files and that the way she handled that information led to her death."

"It sounds possible. She was a clever girl. She lived in one of our empty dorm rooms and no one knew it. She took a novice's habit and used it for her own purposes. She stole Tina's handbag so she could pose as a novice. I'm sure what you're suggesting would not have been out of the question."

"I'd like your permission to look through your files while I'm here." My voice almost gave out as I made my request. It was so preposterous, I didn't have to listen for the answer.

"You know I can't do that, Chris. You know that I would never disclose personal information to anyone."

"I had to ask."

She smiled. "Just on the chance that you had caught me in a very weak moment."

"Why do I think you have a good idea who killed Randy Collins?"

"Because you think the answer lies in my files. I would guess it isn't there."

"But it might provide an opening," I said.

"Because of the nature of this murder, I know many of the facts that you usually come to tell me when you need help. So let's turn things around. Tell me what I don't know—or what you don't know, the tantalizing little things that just don't seem to fit."

"How Randy got to my house," I said. "She told me she took the train and then a taxi from the Oakwood station. No cab driver has a record or a memory of driving her from the station to anywhere near my house. She was dressed like a novice. No driver would forget her."

"And what do you think?"

"I think it's possible she walked. It would be a long walk and she would have had to ask directions. But it's more likely that someone drove her."

"That sounds right. Especially if no one saw her. She would be hard to forget in the habit."

"There was no car or taxi outside when I opened the door."

"She might have waited till it left," Joseph said. "Or she might have asked to be let off around the corner."

"And the person who drove her may have come back on Sunday morning and killed her."

"Why?"

"Because she knew something about him. Because she blackmailed him."

"It certainly makes sense, especially if Randy's birth mother knew nothing about any of this."

"There's another thing," I said, stepping into more forbidden territory. "You weren't at mass at St. Stephen's that Sunday morning."

"That's true. I attended mass somewhere else."

I didn't expect her to tell me where or why, but I wanted her to know that this was one of those puzzling little problems, and that I believed there was a connection to Randy in Joseph's absence from mass at the St. Stephen's chapel. "I believe you know who the killer is," I said.

"I don't know either firsthand or secondhand. I wasn't there and no one has told me he was the killer or that he knows who the killer was."

Which didn't answer the question I had alluded to. "I understand."

"What do you understand?"

"That you would never break a confidence."

"And that's as true for anyone I know as it is for you, Chris."

"I have to go," I said. "I want to see if I can locate your brother."

"Please give him my love," Katherine Bailey said.

25

I called information for a number for Tim Bailey at the address Joseph had given me. I expected to be told that there was no one by that name at that address, but to my surprise, the operator gave me a number. I waited till late afternoon to dial it.

The voice that answered was that of an older woman. I asked for Timothy Bailey.

"They're still gone," she said.

I noticed the "they." "When do you expect him back?"

"I don't know. I don't think he has any plans to come back right now."

"Do you know where he is?"

"I guess he's still in Alaska."

"Do you have a number for him there?"

"I must have it somewhere. Is this some kind of emergency?"

"It's a family matter. It's important that I speak to him."

"Just a minute." The phone was put down with a clatter. She stayed away for about a minute, then picked up again. "Here it is." She read the number off to me.

"Is he working there?" I asked.

"Well, I certainly hope so."

"May I ask who you are?"

"I'm his mother-in-law."

"I see. Thank you. I'll try to call him at this number."

"Who are you?"

"This is Chris."

"OK, Chris. Nice talking to you."

As I hung up I thought that I had come further than I had expected. I was still a little surprised that Tim Bailey was even listed in the phone book, especially at an address that he obviously hadn't lived at for some time and had no immediate plans to return to. Eddie was happy working on some toys, so I picked up the phone again and dialed the number in Alaska the woman had given me.

"Hello?" It was a woman's voice and I heard a dog barking somewhere.

"Mrs. Bailey?"

"Yes."

"I'd like to talk to Tim, please."

"Just a minute."

I assumed, since it was after five on the east coast, that it was four hours earlier where I was calling. Still, even in the middle of the afternoon, he was home.

"Hello?" It was a deep voice with a friendly edge, I thought.

"Is this Tim Bailey?"

"Yeah."

"My name is Chris Bennett. I'm a friend of your sister Katherine."

"Katherine? What's wrong? What's happened?" His voice went from easy to worried.

"Katherine is fine. All your sisters are fine."

"OK. I'm glad to hear it. How did you find me?"

"Your mother-in-law gave me your number."

"Is that what she called herself?"

I didn't respond to the question. "Mr. Bailey, I have a couple of questions I'd like to ask you about some things that happened a number of years ago."

"I don't follow you."

"About twenty years ago, Katherine took a year off from the convent and went back to Ohio."

"Yeah. When a cousin of ours was sick."

"That's right, B.G. I talked to his son recently. During that year, you moved out of your mother's house."

"Around that time. I don't remember exactly. What's this all about?"

"During that year a woman gave birth in Good Samaritan Hospital to a baby girl that she gave up for adoption." I paused, but he said nothing. "She used the name Katherine Bailey. I think you may know who that woman was."

"My sister is a nun. She's never had any children."

"I know that. What I'm saying is that another woman used her name to disguise the fact that she had a baby without being married."

"I don't know what you're talking about."

"I think you do. The telephone number the woman gave the adoption agency was the number of the phone in your apartment."

"How did you dig this up?"

"Do you know who the woman is, Mr. Bailey?"

"Yeah, I know who she is."

I took an immense breath. Sometimes I can hardly

believe how far I have traveled, metaphorically speaking, from the beginning almost to the end, in this case from a girl in a novice's habit lying dead on the ground near a chopped-down tree to a man in Alaska who was her father. "And you know she used your sister's name in the hospital and with the adoption agency?"

"I know. I'm sorry. We were young, she was pregnant, I couldn't see myself married much less a father, and this seemed a way out for her. No one would ever know and she could go back to her life without her family being upset, all of that stuff."

"I appreciate your honesty, Mr. Bailey."

"Does Katherine know this?"

"Yes. We don't know who the woman was, but it doesn't matter."

"You want her name?"

"No. I just wanted to clear up the use of Katherine's name."

"Tell her I'm sorry."

"I will. And she asked me to send you her love."

I called Joseph and told her quickly what I had learned. She asked for the phone number in Alaska and I gave it to her. It was a short conversation. I had Eddie's dinner to put together as well as ours and there was nothing further to discuss. The mystery of Randy's parentage had been solved. I would never know who Randy's mother was, but I didn't need to. Her parentage and her murder were separate, except that it was her search for her mother that had led to her demise.

When Jack and I talked later, I told him where my thinking was leading me now. "Randy spent a week or two in and around St. Stephen's. During that time she befriended Tina Richmond, stole her purse, took a novice's habit from the laundry, and, we're both pretty sure, went through Joseph's files. She found me there and decided I might be able to help her approach Joseph, although I think she got cold feet about that. She told me she had come here by train and taken a taxi from the station."

"But none of the drivers admit driving her here."

"So let's assume that someone at St. Stephen's drove her."

"You mean one of the nuns?" I could hear the shock in his voice.

"Maybe a nun, maybe someone who works at the convent. There's a cook, her helper, the groundsman, and some other people who work there. Some of the nuns have cars. The people who work there have cars. Randy could have asked one of them—maybe paid them—to drive her here."

"That's a lot of people to interview. Do you know which nuns own cars?"

I shook my head. "Randy needed two things, a ride to Oakwood and information about Joseph. Maybe one person gave her both, maybe it was two separate people. She wanted to find out who Joseph was, where she came from, whether she could have had a child, things the nuns wouldn't ordinarily tell her. I'm going to sit down and review every person I can think of at St. Stephen's and see if I can figure out which one might be blackmailable."

"Just by thinking about it?"

"As a first step anyway."

"Hey, if you can do this all in your head, I know a thousand detectives who'd like to get in on your method.

They'll put you on the squad payroll. Their case clearance rate will skyrocket."

"Let's see if I succeed first."

"Good luck, kiddo."

That's the way I felt. I was sure of one thing: No one would gossip about Joseph to a stranger. After dinner I started writing down names as they came to me. As each name appeared on my sheet, I was faced with the impossibility of considering that that woman could have been blackmailed and, even worse, could have fired a bullet into Randy Collins.

There were the elderly nuns in the Villa. It was crazy to think that a woman—a nun—in her seventies or eighties could have been part of this. There were the active nuns, all of whom I knew, none of whom I disliked, mistrusted, or feared. Angela was a friend. Grace had embroidered the beautiful chapel cloth that my mother-in-law had given to the convent as a gift in honor of our marriage. I considered one after the other, trying to think of gossip I might have heard, a hint of a possible scandal. What kind of scandal can a woman who has lived in a convent for twenty or thirty years become involved in?

I pushed away the sheet of paper and started another. Harold the groundsman. Harold has dedicated his life to the convent. He is grumpy and difficult, but there is no question he loves his job and reveres the nuns.

I knew nothing about the cook, Mrs. Halsey. What had Joseph known when she hired her? Maybe there was something there. And then there was Mrs. Halsey's assistant, Jennifer, who had recognized Randy's picture but had not seen her wearing the habit. Jennifer was close to Randy's age. If she didn't have her own car, maybe she had borrowed her mother's and taken twenty or thirty dollars from Randy to drive her to Oakwood. She would have to work a number of hours to earn that much money.

I started feeling encouraged. Maybe this would prove fruitful. And maybe, instead of calling Joseph tomorrow to ask about these two women, I would ask Angela. Angela had her fingers on the pulse of the convent.

I sat back and pushed myself to think of other people that might have known personal information about Joseph or who had a car, or both. Some kind of cleaning service came in to clean up the dormitory and the classrooms. I would have to get their names.

And then it hit me. There were men working on renovating dormitory rooms. I had met them and they had denied knowing Randy, but people don't always tell the truth. Randy could have met them, especially as she was squatting on the same floor in the dorm that they were working on. Perhaps one of those men had driven her to Oakwood. I tried to recall how old those men were and how many there had been.

"You getting somewhere?" Jack asked, looking up from the newspaper.

"Maybe."

"Got a coupla nuns who're murder suspects?"

"Don't be nasty. I'm thinking of workmen in the dormitory."

"OK. Sounds a lot better than a nun."

"He could have driven her down here that Thursday afternoon and dropped her off at the corner."

"Why'd he come back on Sunday?"

"I don't know yet."

"Promises, promises."

"Maybe he was going to drive her back to St. Stephen's on Sunday and he came early."

"Who did Sister Joseph meet on Sunday morning?"

"I have no idea. Maybe she just decided to go to mass somewhere else."

"It's a loose end, Chris."

"Only if I can't put my finger on a killer."

In the morning I called the convent. Angela answered and I asked her what she knew about the men working in the dormitory.

"I've never seen them, Kix. Joseph hired them and they've been around for a while. They should be finishing up soon."

"Are they there today?"

"They should be."

"Can I talk to Joseph?"

It took a few minutes before they found her and when she answered I could tell she was in or near the kitchen because of the noise.

"Joseph," I said, "I've been thinking about people at St. Stephen's who might have driven Randy to my house. I'd like to come up and talk to the workmen working in the dormitory."

"They're here today. That won't be a problem."

I said I would leave very shortly and would bring Eddie along. Before I left, I called and let Jack know where I was going.

"You better watch yourself," he warned. "I don't need a hostage situation with my wife and son as hostages."

I promised I'd keep Eddie away from my suspects, which didn't satisfy him very much, and we took off.

Two of the nuns in the Villa took Eddie for a walk while Joseph and I went to the dorm. Upstairs the men were working, talking loudly enough that we heard them as we climbed the stairs. When they saw Joseph, they quieted down and became very deferential.

"This is my friend Mrs. Brooks," Joseph said. "We would like to ask you gentlemen some questions, one at a time so that we don't stop your work."

"You're the lady with the picture of the dead girl," one of the men said.

"That's right."

"We told you we didn't see her."

"There are other things we want to talk to you about," Joseph said. "Mr. Grassly, would you like to come with me?"

The man who had just spoken put down a tool and wiped his hands on his white cotton overalls. He followed us to the room Randy had lived in and Joseph unlocked the door.

"I'll wait outside," she said. "Take your time."

"What's this about?" Grassly said. "We told you we never saw her."

He seemed a lot more nervous than when I had spoken to him eleven days earlier. "Mr. Grassly, I think you may have driven that girl somewhere about two weeks ago."

"I never saw her. I don't know who she is."

"What kind of car do you drive?" I opened my notebook and took out a pen.

"I don't have to tell you that. The police were here last week. We all talked to them. We told them we didn't see her."

"That was last week. I know a lot more today than I did then. I think she came and asked you men for a ride. Mr. Grassly, this girl was murdered. I need to know how she got from St. Stephen's to the next place she went." Having made a terrible mistake in my questioning of Barbara Phillips, I was being extra careful now not to give anything away.

He stared at me. He was sitting on the desk chair and I was on the bed. Nothing of Randy's was in the room. It was an unlived-in dormitory room, waiting for a student to move in.

"She came to us," he said. "She said she needed a lift, she would pay us. I said, 'OK, I'll take you.'"

"Where did you take her?" My voice was almost soft. I felt as though, if I weren't careful, some fragile bond between us would break.

"Down almost to the city."

"To where?" He had caught me off guard.

"To the city, you know, New York. She wanted to go to New York but I wouldn't take her all the way. I hate driving in New York. I found a subway station, must've been on Broadway, way up in Manhattan. I let her off there and I got back on the highway and came back. I never saw her again."

"What day was that?"

"I gotta think." He pulled a little booklet out of his pants pocket. It was one of those agendas that you get free from stationery stores or banks. He flipped a few pages that were dirty with thumbprints. "It coulda been that Thursday two weeks ago."

"What time did you drive her in?"

"After work."

"And you think it was Thursday." Randy had shown up on my doorstep that Thursday in the early evening.

"Maybe Wednesday. Yeah, I bet it was Wednesday. I hadda get something to take home that day. I did it on the way back."

"Were any of the other men with you?" I asked.

"Nah. I was driving the truck. The others had their cars, at least one of them did. I took her myself."

"Did she tell you where she was going?"

"She said New York. That's all she told me."

"What did you do the Sunday after you took the girl to New York?"

"Sunday?" He seemed confused. "I don't know what I did Sunday. I went to church. Maybe I watched some baseball in the afternoon."

"You didn't meet anybody that day?"

"I told you: I never saw that girl again. I never heard anything about her till you came and showed us that picture."

"Thank you, Mr. Grassly."

I don't know what I expected but certainly not that the first man I questioned would turn out to be the one I was looking for. I was so used to finding my source at the end of the trail rather than at the beginning that I must have looked confused myself as I left the room. Grassly went back to work, somewhat deflated. Joseph was talking to two students, apparently having a pleasant conversation. They were all beaming. When she saw me, she gave each girl a pat on the shoulder and crossed the hall to where I was standing.

"He drove her," I said.

"To your house?"

"To upper Manhattan. He wouldn't go any farther. He hates Manhattan traffic."

"Where does that leave you?" she asked.

"With a whole new idea," I said.

26

Maybe I should have felt discouraged. My brilliant thought had not panned out as I had hoped, but it had taken me halfway to an answer. It was the second half, the dark part, that had to be illuminated. I just needed the source of the light.

I hadn't even stayed to have lunch. Eddie had been given his and as soon as I started the car, he fell asleep. Aside from the need to stay alert on the road, I was free to think.

It was possible that Grassly had lied. But all he knew about me was my name. He had no idea where I lived unless Randy had told him, which I doubted. She knew how to keep things to herself and he was a stranger who needed to know nothing. If he had driven her to Oakwood, I thought it was very likely he would have told me.

When he said he didn't like to drive in the city, it had rung true. If you're used to suburban or country driving, navigating the streets of New York can be more than a challenge; it can be a downright threat. I've had my share of narrow misses on the streets and avenues of the big city.

So what did the situation look like now? Randy took a lift from Mr. Grassly, who let her off near a subway station. She could have stayed overnight with a friend from school or, for all I knew, she could have sat on a park bench till Thursday morning. But why had she gone to New York? As it happened, taking a train from New York to Oakwood was a lot easier and more direct than doing the same from St. Stephen's. *But no one had seen her at the Oakwood station.* So maybe someone in New York had driven her to Oakwood.

But that would exclude all the nuns (thank the good Lord) and all the other people based at St. Stephen's. And it wasn't very logical to think that a college friend would turn around and kill her. It had to be someone else. Somehow it had to be connected with those files that Joseph, properly, refused to let me see.

When it came to me, my head almost exploded.

Eddie woke up as the car came to a stop at our house and I carried him in while he went through the slow process of becoming fully awake. We sat at the kitchen table and he drank some milk as I ate some cheese and carrot sticks to ease my hunger pangs.

"I want to make a phone call, Eddie, and then we'll go outside and play."

He hopped off the chair with my help and got his own brightly colored telephone and started to make his own calls. I just hoped that whoever he was talking to would keep him occupied for a few more minutes.

Jack answered and asked how it had gone. He seemed surprised that my guess about Randy getting a ride anywhere had been right.

"But it wasn't to Oakwood and I think someone in New York may have driven her up on Thursday."

"Name your suspects."

"I only have one, the former nun I visited while Randy was still here, Jane Cirillo."

"Interesting. What led you there?"

"Randy may have read something damning about her in Joseph's file. She may have tried to blackmail Jane into telling what she knew or suspected about Joseph, without realizing Jane would have told her anything she wanted to know without being coerced. Jane doesn't have any warm fuzzy feelings about St. Stephen's."

"And then you came down a couple of days later and Jane figured Randy was telling all anyway."

"Right."

"So what can I do for you? I gather this isn't a 'Hi honey, how're you doing?' call."

"I want to know if Jane owns a car."

"OK. How 'bout a licensed handgun, same caliber as our friendly neighbor's?"

"That, too."

"I'll get back to you."

I knew it was a long shot but all the facts fit. Jane had left the convent under a cloud and the reason for her departure might well be in the file. It must have seemed much more than a coincidence to her to have two people come to her in the space of two or three days and ask about Joseph's whereabouts twenty years ago, but in truth, Randy and I had been drawn to her from very different directions. Randy had found something in Jane's file that could be used against her. I was merely looking for someone who had been at the convent twenty years ago and wouldn't mind gossiping about it.

But there it was: Randy appeared on Jane's doorstep, asked her questions about Joseph, and got a ride to my house the next evening. Then, only about twenty-four hours later, there I was asking some of the same questions. It made it look as though Randy had gotten what she wanted from Jane and then gone ahead and spilled her secrets anyway.

Jack came home with the news I was waiting for. "She owns a car," he said. "So far so good for your assumptions. But no handgun. That doesn't mean she doesn't have one, just that she hasn't registered one. She could have picked up a gun in another state and brought it back to New York illegally. It wouldn't be the first time."

"So Randy could have knocked on Jane's door on Wednesday night and found out what she wanted to know about Joseph. Then Jane could have driven Randy up here on Thursday."

"Jane Cirillo works," Jack said. "I did a little checking. She has a job at a bank in Manhattan."

"That's why Randy arrived Thursday evening. Maybe Jane has flexible hours and took Friday off when I drove in to see her."

"That's possible. But working for a bank, if she did any funny stuff at the convent, that could lose her her job if it became known."

"And that's exactly the point. She must have done some 'funny stuff' and there's a record of it in Joseph's file."

"You know, you don't have enough to get a warrant, but you've got enough to make me think you're on the right track."

"Me, too."

"But I can't let you go see her alone, Chris. I don't mean to act the heavy, but if you're right about her, this is a shrewd woman who owns a deadly weapon that she might easily use for the second time if you're alone with her in her apartment."

"I could take her to lunch," I said. "With you at the next table."

"Joe Fox and me at the next table. This is his case, whatever you think of him."

To be honest, I didn't think much of him, but Jack was right. I couldn't chance being alone in an apartment with a killer who very likely still had her weapon. "If you're there, I'll accept it."

"Let me give him a call."

It took a little doing, a couple of calls to Jane, one to ask if she would join me for lunch the next day, the second, after talking to Joe Fox who set it up with the restaurant, to tell her where we would meet.

Elsie took Eddie. The farther away from criminals that I can keep him, the better off we'll be. Jack and I drove into the city earlier than our appointment so that Jack and Joe Fox could look around the restaurant and be seated when I arrived. I knew from talking to Jack that detectives like to get to a meet early, check out the area, especially the doors and windows inside and out. It cuts down on surprises if the meet goes bad or gets ugly.

Jane had not met either of them so they could sit in the open without being recognized. Jack went into the restaurant at noon. I had told Jane we would meet at twelve-fifteen. At ten after, I went in and took my seat, leaving empty the one closer to Joe Fox who was at the next table, his back to ours.

Jane was late but not very. She was less casually dressed than the first time I had seen her. Today I could believe she worked in a bank Monday through Friday.

She sat down and ordered a drink and we exchanged a little small talk.

"Was I any help to you last time we met?" she asked finally, sipping a whiskey and soda.

"A lot. I really appreciated your taking the time. I wanted to ask you a few more questions. I understand Randy Collins came to see you."

Her face clouded. "Never heard the name. Is that a man or a woman?"

And then I remembered. Randy had been playing a part the last days of her life. "I meant Tina Richmond."

"Tina. Yeah. I did run into a girl named Tina. What's the connection?"

"I think she was also interested in Sister Joseph."

"Mmm."

"Did you meet with Sister Joseph the Sunday before last?" I asked.

"Did she tell you that?"

"She didn't tell me anything. She didn't attend mass at St. Stephen's that day and she's refused to say where she was. I think she met with you."

"Why would she do that?" The smile had gone. Jane was on guard now.

"Because you called her and said you wanted to talk to her. You thought she had broken a promise to you."

"What's this about, Chris? What's the point of these questions?"

"I need to find the truth."

"The truth? About what Joseph did on a Sunday morning? About where Joseph spent a year of her life when you were a kid?"

"I know about what she did twenty years ago. I need

to know what happened the Sunday before last. I'd like to know where you were."

"Sleeping in my own little bed."

"I don't think so. I think you met the girl who called herself Tina and you shot her. And I think after that you met Sister Joseph and told her she had betrayed you."

She stared at me over our appetizers, her fork in her hand, her eyes cold and hard. "What business is it of yours who I met, where I went, what I did?"

"It's my business because that girl ended up dead down the street from my house. And she was a guest in my home at the time."

"Next thing you'll tell me she had an ax in her hand."

My heart did something crazy. "Why did she chop down the tree?" I asked.

"She was one of those adorable little girls who wanted to set the world straight. She told me some crazy story about that tree and the trouble it was causing for two families. She could set everything right if she just got rid of it. That's how I felt about her."

It was chilling hearing her say that. "So she chopped it down."

"I turned the corner and there she was. She had called me the night before and told me she had gotten herself in a mess, nothing was working out, whoever she was staying with didn't believe her story, and she was out of money. Money was what she wanted, of course. I said I'd meet her early in the morning and give her some and said she'd better get out of my life. But that never works, you know."

"Blackmailers don't give up," I said.

"Never."

"She would have. It wasn't the *money* she wanted; it was information."

"I told her what I knew."

"So you called Joseph and set up a meeting for later that morning."

"You bet. You were right. She had betrayed me."

"I don't think Joseph has ever betrayed anyone in her life. I think the girl who called herself Tina found some things out about you that she had no right to know and she used that information to her advantage."

"That's what you say."

It was what I knew. "So you shot the girl to keep her from telling what she knew about you."

"I would have lost my job. I would never have gotten another one. I might have been prosecuted."

"What did you do, Jane?" I had a few ideas but I wanted to hear the truth. I didn't think Joseph would ever tell me.

"You might say I robbed the poorbox. Let's leave it at that. You'd be surprised what goes on up there. I could tell you—"

"I don't want to hear," I said angrily. Then I said, "The poorbox," more to myself than to her. Surely she had not murdered Randy over something so minor, albeit unethical. I tried to think back. I had been at St. Stephen's when Sister Jane Anthony disappeared and no one would talk about it. How many years ago had it been? Eight? Nine? I couldn't put my finger on it. And then I remembered. I had gone to the chapel one morning to pray and had noticed something amiss. Several beautiful old icons were missing. At least one was gold with jeweled eyes. I had intended to ask what had happened to them but with my busy schedule, the day had passed and when I went to the chapel for evening prayers, everything was back in place. I had assumed some cleaning had been done, but now I knew better.

"You took the statues," I said. "The gold one with the jewels and all the beautiful old silver pieces."

"You have a good memory." She drained her glass.

"And Joseph knew it was you and made you put it all back."

"She caught me red-handed. She said she wouldn't turn me over to the police if I signed a statement saying what I had done and got the hell out of St. Stephen's before noon. She said if she ever heard that I'd been involved in felonious activity—that's how she put it— she'd haul out my sworn statement and turn it over to the authorities. She had one of the nuns witness my signing."

"And then she put the statement in the Sister Jane Anthony file," I said.

"I don't know where she put it. I had an uncle who got me a job where you've got to be squeaky clean and Joseph wrote a letter of recommendation that I'd been a nun at the convent for so-and-so many years and had left of my own volition. Even without the usual accolades, I got the job. My uncle was an officer and who could quarrel with a nun's cloistered life?"

"I suppose Joseph filed a copy of her recommendation, too."

"And then," Jane went on, ignoring my comment, "this Tina shows up a couple of weeks ago and starts asking questions. She's a novice at St. Stephen's, she tells me, and there are things she needs to know about Sister Joseph. I told her I had nothing to say and she pulls out stuff about my past that I couldn't believe. She knew where I worked. She knew what I'd done. The only way she could have found all that out was from Joseph. Or maybe from the nun who witnessed my signature, but I don't think she really knew what was going on."

"Joseph never told anyone, Jane," I said. "She never even told the police that she'd seen you that Sunday morning. She was as good as her word."

"You think this Tina went through the convent files?"

"I'm sure of it. What did you tell her?"

"The same thing I told you, that Joseph had taken a year off a long time ago. That I didn't think she had boyfriends. Then this Tina asked me for some money so she could take the train somewhere. I told her I'd drive her. After work, I drove her up to a place called Oakwood."

"And she knocked on my door."

"Small world," Jane said.

We had begun eating. I was being very careful not to look at the table with Jack and the detective but I sensed they were aware of what was going on at my table. Detective Fox had a canvas bag slung over the back of his chair and I thought it was likely he was recording at least Jane's side of the conversation.

"When did Tina call you back?" I asked.

"Some time on Saturday, I think. Nothing was going right. She was out of money. We've all heard it before. I didn't like where this was going."

"Where did you get the gun, Jane?"

"I got it. What difference does it make where?"

"Why didn't you shoot Sister Joseph, too?" I asked. "When you saw her that Sunday morning. You thought she betrayed you. Why did you let her go on living?"

She smiled a little at that. "I assumed she'd left word where she was going. She's a nun, after all. She couldn't just get up and leave the convent and go off somewhere without telling someone where she'd gone. If she turned up dead or missing and my name and address were on her desk, I was in big trouble."

That was good thinking. It was even possible Joseph had left such a note on her desk, and then destroyed it when she came back. "How did you come to be home the day I dropped in on you?"

"Sheer luck. I had planned to take that day off a long time ago. On any other weekday, I'd've been at the bank. But when you started asking me the same questions Tina had, I had to believe she had told you about me. How else could you have found out?"

"She never told me," I said, feeling great sadness. "I just happened to think of you and I wanted to talk to someone who had been at the convent twenty years ago and who might be inclined to open up."

"I guess it's too bad," she said. "I didn't have anything against her, except that I didn't want her ruining my life. As for you, don't even think of telling this wild story to anyone else. The gun doesn't exist. And after I have my last bite, I'm gone."

"I don't think so, Miss Cirillo," Joe Fox said. He had gotten up from his chair and come to our table. He flashed his shield and said, "Keep your hands where I can see them. I'm placing you under arrest. You have the right to remain silent."

27

I sat there for a long time after they left, my heart throbbing. I was glad it was over but it had been traumatic. Jack moved over to my table and held my hand while I tried to calm down.

"Did you hear?" I asked.

"Almost nothing. Joe had a recorder in the bag on the chair. It should have picked up everything. By the way, he said he intends to go to St. Stephen's and apologize personally to Sister Joseph."

"He should." I drank most of my ice water.

"Maybe you'd like something a little stronger than that."

"I don't think so. I just wish it hadn't turned out this way for Randy Collins. She picked the wrong person to question. It's terrible that a life ended because of a bad choice."

"She say anything about the tree?"

"She did. It was Randy's way of trying to remove the cause of the trouble. She thought if she just got rid of it, the parties would have to come to an agreement."

"She was right. Want some coffee?"

"I just want to go home. I have to call Joseph. There's our waitress. Let's get the bill."

"Joe took care of it in advance. This is a free lunch."

"I thought there was no such thing."

"There isn't. Think about what it cost you."

I didn't feel up to it.

Joseph drove down the next day at our invitation. It was two weeks since Mother's Day, two weeks since I had called her to come and identify Randy's body. On this day, I took my cousin Gene to mass and then brought him back to the house for dinner with all of us.

When Gene saw Joseph, old memories surfaced. "You're a brown lady," he said.

"Yes, I am. I'm a nun."

"Kix is a brown lady."

"Well, she used to be. That's how I know her."

"Two brown ladies," he said with a big smile. "One, two." Then he went back to playing with Eddie.

Joseph and I set the table and then got out of Jack's way while he finished making our dinner. Two weeks ago had been Mother's Day and he had made a treat we had not been able to enjoy fully.

"I'm sure you understand that I couldn't tell you what I knew of Jane Anthony Cirillo," Joseph said. "I had given her my word and I had no reason to believe that she had ever been in trouble again."

"You don't have to explain to me. But your absence at mass on Mother's Day created a lot of questions. I suppose she called you and accused you of betraying her trust."

"She did. We met about halfway between New York and the convent and by the time you called to ask me to come and identify the body of a novice, I was back home. I couldn't believe there was a connection between Jane's problem and the mysterious girl who was killed on your block. Jane wasn't specific about who had told her the facts of her dismissal from St. Stephen's, but in thinking about it, I realized that if she heard it from someone she believed to be a novice, she must have thought we were all talking about it, that it was common gossip. I can see why she was angry."

"I'm really sorry I upset your family so much," I said. "I'm sure Hope will never forgive me."

"I've spoken to her. And I've talked to my brother for the first time in twenty years, Chris. If anything good has come of this, it's that we've all resumed our family ties. I think he's going to allow himself to be persuaded to visit us."

"I suppose he feels bad about the deception."

"He does, but it didn't hurt me and it allowed some poor young woman to save face. I hope, whoever she is, that she's happy."

"And I'm sorry, too, that you felt you had to tell me facts about your own life that you obviously wanted to keep to yourself."

"What difference does it make? I know who I am."

And that's the way we left it. We had a great meal and a lot of fun that afternoon. The day was long and Joseph left while it was still light. She called the next day to say that Detective Fox had traveled to the convent to offer his apologies to her, apologies she had accepted, graciously, I'm sure.

The gun that killed Randy Collins was never found, but the recording Detective Fox made in the restaurant was loud and clear. Jane confessed to everything in the police station.

The Greiners agreed, finally, to pay for the Kovaks' driveway and the Kovaks reciprocated by buying a beautiful young tree and planting it well inside the Greiners' property line. Only its shade will ever reach the Kovaks' driveway.

It was probably several weeks later, when the heat of late spring started to entice us into the Oakwood pool, that I thought again about the involved relationships in Joseph's family. They were all related to Randy. Tim was her natural father, his sisters were her aunts.

And then there was Cousin B.G. I had thought that B.G. and Joseph were first cousins related by blood. But as it turned out, there was no blood relationship between them at all. It made me wonder. And wondering made me smile.

In Conversation. . .

LEE HARRIS AND
CHRISTINE BENNETT

LEE: **Chris, my name is Lee Harris and I write a mystery series with you as the main character. I have a few questions I'd like to ask you.**

CHRIS: So that's what you look like! I expected you to be much older and to wear glasses on your nose. You're much better looking than I thought you'd be. Could you tell me what holiday you're doing next?

LEE: **Well, thank you, Chris. Uh, I think I'm the one who should ask the questions here. What I'd like to know most of all is what particular gift or talent of yours you believe helps you to solve these mysteries.**

CHRIS: It's knowing that each of us is the sum of our experiences, that we weren't born yesterday, that what happened to us a long time ago affects us today, possibly even more than what we have just experienced.

LEE: **What else gives you an edge over the police?**

CHRIS: I dig deeper in areas where they might merely make a phone call. I remember when I was looking into the disappearance of the woman at the Thanksgiving Day parade, and I went to her former employer and asked people who worked there about her. Jack—my husband— said the cops would have called, gotten some surface information, and left it at that. They had pretty much given up ever finding her when that case dropped in my lap. I couldn't have done it without interviewing the people at the ad agency. They were the key.

LEE: **Yes, I remember that one. You certainly are a digger. Tell me, with all you have to do—your husband, your little boy, the class you teach, your concern about civic affairs, your cousin Gene—isn't it an imposition on your time to solve homicides?**

CHRIS: Quite the opposite, Lee. For me, it's a gift. Every homicide is different. Every victim has a unique history. While I hate the idea of killing, I become engrossed in finding out why it happened, why someone became so angry, so distraught, so out of control that he could take away a life. Trying to solve a murder is a privilege for me.

LEE: **You certainly have a very positive attitude. I've noticed, too, that you believe that if you play fair with people you question, that they'll play fair with you and tell you the truth—but that doesn't always happen. Do you have any problem—I mean spiritually—when you don't tell the truth yourself?**

CHRIS: I do, but I'm convinced the cause is worth it. There's probably a time in every case when I have to tell a white lie to get someone to respond. I remind myself that there's a murderer out there who must be caught and I've got the best chance of catching him. I'm not saying it's right, but I am saying I do it if I have to. Don't you wear glasses at all? You're taking notes without them.

LEE: **Only for distance. Do you think you'll keep teaching the same poetry class?**

CHRIS: You know, that's something I've been thinking about. I really enjoy it. The students are always different—and that's what makes it such a pleasure. But I might see if there's something else I could teach next year. I always enjoy a challenge.

LEE: **That seems to sum up your work as an amateur sleuth, that you enjoy a challenge. Is that true?**

CHRIS: I believe it is. As I said before, every case is different; they're all unique. And I learn from each one. Don't you get bored writing about the same people all the time?

LEE: **Actually, every mystery is different. Every mystery is unique. And I love a challenge, too. Tell me, do you think you'll ever learn to cook? I mean, really well.**

CHRIS: I don't think so. Jack is such a good cook, and my friend Melanie is, too. I don't mind getting down in the dirt and weeding my garden or going through my students' papers with a fine-tooth comb, but somehow cooking just doesn't excite me.

LEE: **One last question: Where would you like to go from here? Is there some kind of murder you'd like to get your teeth into?**

CHRIS: Maybe one where everything points to a person that I know in my heart couldn't have done it.

LEE: **But what if he did? Or she?**

CHRIS: Please don't do that to me, Lee. . . . You know, I really love the way you wear your hair. Do you do it yourself, or does someone do it for you?

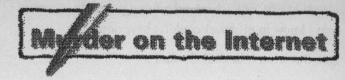

Ballantine mysteries are on the Web!

Read about your favorite Ballantine authors and
upcoming books in our monthly electronic newsletter
MURDER ON THE INTERNET, at
www.randomhouse.com/BB/MOTI

Including:

- 🕷What's new in the stores
- 🕷Previews of upcoming books for the next four months
- 🕷In-depth interviews with mystery authors and
  publishing insiders
- 🕷Calendars of signings and readings for Ballantine
  mystery authors
- 🕷Profiles of mystery authors
- 🕷Excerpts from new mysteries

To subscribe to MURDER ON THE INTERNET,
please send an e-mail to
join-mystery@list.randomhouse.com
with "subscribe" as the body of the message. (Don't
use the quotes.) You will receive the next issue as
soon as it's available.

Find out more about whodunit! For sample
chapters from current and upcoming Ballantine
mysteries, visit us at
www.randomhouse.com/BB/mystery